COLBY

TUCKER'S PRIDE BOOK 5

KATHI S. BARTON

This is a work of fiction. Names, characters, places, and incidents are products of the author's imagination or are used fictitiously and are not to be construed as real. Any resemblance to actual events, locations, organizations, or persons, living or dead, is entirely coincidental.

World Castle Publishing, LLC
Pensacola, Florida
Copyright © 2025 Kathi S. Barton
Hardback ISBN: 9798263139797
Paperback ISBN: 9798891264656
eBook ISBN: 9798891264663
First Edition World Castle Publishing, LLC, September 8, 2025
http://www.worldcastlepublishing.com

Licensing Notes

Cover: Cover Designs by Karen
Editor: Karen Fuller

Prologue

Emma backed her trailer up to the bay doors and waited for the signal that her locks were in place. Once they were, she put her truck into park and turned it off. Getting out, she had her gloves on and was ready to lock things in place when her mom said her name. She told her that she had a phone call.

"Take a message, and I'll call them back. We're behind enough on this load, and I want to get out of here as soon as they get me empty." Mom said that she'd do that, and Emma finished locking down the trailer so that the people on the inside could work on getting things done. She hated to unload or load at this center.

This was the third time this month that their scheduled time had been put back. The first time, it had been only an hour. This time, it was nearly seven. She didn't have time to pussy foot around with a center if they didn't get their shit together. It was nearly dark when she decided to get into her bed and eat something with her mom. They'd been traveling together since her dad died five years ago, and it had been working out well for the two of them.

"What is it you've made us?" Mom handed her a plate of still steaming spaghetti and meatballs with garlic bread. "This is a bit much, don't you think?"

"Well, we had plans to have dinner out tonight, and I had my heart set on Italian. But this place has screwed that all up. Again. Besides, it's not that much to throw some frozen meatballs into the pot with the noodles. Not all that good but rib-sticking." They ate in silence for a few minutes before her mom spoke again. "I heard from your grandpa. He said that the real estate agent showed the house to a couple today. I hope they can sell it. I'm sick of paying taxes on the place when we don't even live there."

Her father had passed away a month and a half after the house had been completely paid off. Even with the mortgage that he'd borrowed against the house for her semi, which was now fully paid. From the beginning, her parents had supported her, and now that she was free of any kind of payments to the bank, the profit that she made went a bit further when paying bills. The house being sold would save them a bit more. The two of them were making a profit now, but without the monthly taxes, it would be easier to bank more.

"Don't forget to call that person back. I think that it was the same person as before, Denver Tucker." She said she'd call him as soon as she was finished eating. "Are they the ones that I sent all that paperwork to when they were looking for full-time drivers?"

"Yes. They're opening a distribution center along the coast. It'll be nice to be at home at night. I know we'd have to buy us a place, but it won't have to be as big as the place we had back home." The house had been in their family for generations, but neither she nor her mom was all that sentimental about the place. In fact, they both hated living there after her dad had died. "Maybe we can get us a little condo that has a couple of bedrooms, so we don't have to do yard crap either."

"I'd like to have a crafting room. And a big kitchen. Well, not big, but big enough that I could cook some cookies when I want." They had talked about this before, finding a driving job so that she could be home nightly. Her mom had gotten her driver's license to drive one of the big rigs, but she didn't care for it. It had helped a great deal, her knowing how to drive to keep them on track when working. "You know how much it would cost to get us something smaller to go to the store in. I don't care for driving this sucker to the grocery store when we need something."

The two of them joked around about what they wanted in a house. Mom had said that she wanted a garden so that she could grow her own vegetables. Emma had wanted a garage to hold her rig in. She didn't care if it spent all its time in the weather. They only had nice weather down here where they were working for the most part.

After getting the dishes cleaned up, her mom used regular plates so as not to add to the amount of trash in the world, and it worked out great for them. The two of them only drank bottled water, so there were a lot of empty bottles in the rig when they got to a place to recycle them. Emma thought that the two of them worked well together. After checking to see how much longer they were going to be at this center, she called Denver Tucker.

"We've gone over your application, Ms. Holden,

and it looks like we can work well together. I know you said that your mom didn't want to drive the bigger trucks, but we do have cargo vans that she could drive that would bring in some good money for her as well." She told him that her mom would like that, so long as it wasn't full-time. "I understand that she wants to work part-time, and any time that she can give us will be a blessing. The stores that we're supplying to are smaller stores that families run. But there are approximately seventy of them along the coast that we'll supply."

"That'll be wonderful." He told her that the center was nearly finished on the outside, but the inside was being worked on now. "There will be forty bay doors along with an entire section devoted to the perishable things that will be delivered, such as candy and drinks that can't handle the heat."

"The place we're at now has over a hundred bay doors, but they only use about twenty, which is what makes me late in and out of here. I don't know that they have enough people, or they just don't care about the times, but it's a pain to be here." She shut down her talk about the center where she was working. That didn't bode well to do that to a new employer. "Mom and I will be looking for a place to stay here, too. About where the center is, so that we can be halfway between each delivery."

"There are several condos that you can look into. I can set up a realtor to help you out with that if you want. Also, you will be given an allowance when you have to stay over for whatever reason." She said that she understood there would be times for her to work overnight. "Good.

I'm glad that we're on the same page. As for a starting date, it will be three weeks before the center starts taking in product. Most of the shelves have been put together and are standing. The merge area — the area where all the boxes and products are put on lines to head to the trucks has been running for a few days now, working out the bugs or whatever."

"Three weeks? That's a good deal faster than I thought." He asked her if she was coming to town this week to sign off on paperwork for her new job. "I really thought it would be months yet. I guess you guys know how to get people fired up."

"Yes, it seems that once the land was ready, the rest of it just fell into place. For now, we're only distributing the things for Carol's Plaza, but we might branch out to other stores and shops as we get used to what we're doing. Of course, it helps that we have good drivers like you and your mom on our team, too." She thanked him, embarrassed that he'd say something like that. "If you don't have a return trip, we can have dinner tomorrow night. I understand that you only have one more week to go with the company you — "

"I don't work for a company, Mr. Tucker. I'm an independent driver. Working with you will be under contract, but I work because I want to, not because someone is ordering me to. I'm sorry if that makes a difference to you, but that's what I wanted when I filled out the application to deliver for you and your company." He said that he'd known that but had forgotten. "Thank you. I don't want any misunderstanding going on between us."

"You're right. And neither do we. Thank you very much for reminding me." She told him that she was all right with it, and they moved on. She didn't want to have to only work for one firm. Especially for one that was just starting out. It could mean that she'd not be able to find employment if the company fell through on their promises, and she sort of liked having three meals a day and her truck. "What do you think about having dinner with my family. I will warn you, there are a lot of us, but I think you can hold your own."

She wasn't so sure about that. Emma and her mom had been traveling together for years and had been their only company. But she agreed to have dinner with the family on Friday night. That gave her three days to get something to wear and hang out at the rest stop for truckers. A long, hot shower was going to be on her list of things to get done. What she wouldn't give for a nice big bathtub right now, she thought with a smile.

After leaving the center, they headed to the store. They'd not stopped for supplies in a while, so they were about out of everything. In the bed area, they had a microwave, a small oven, as well as a good-sized refrigerator. All the comforts of home and none of the work that went along with it. Her mom was in charge of the area where she cooked, and the two of them had gotten used to sharing a bed when there was time for them to get a good night's sleep. They got along well and had a wonderful time seeing the country. At least this end of the country.

"What do you think about going to see a movie

tomorrow night?" Mom looked shocked that she'd ask such a question. "It's all right if you don't want to go, Mom. It was just something that I thought you'd enjoy that was about as normal as two people can get."

"How about dinner, too? Oh, it would be nice to have time for both, don't you think?" She told her that she owed her a meal anyway. "I would love to have a date tomorrow night. That'll give us a little bit of time to catch up on things that have been going on. I know how much you dislike having the radio on, but there are newspapers that we can look at, too."

Her mom was teasing her, but she'd been right in saying that she didn't like the radio on. It wasn't just the bad news that seemed to be on every station, but she really did enjoy her quiet time. They would listen to a book if they'd find one that they both thought they'd enjoy, but other than that, the radio was never on.

Picking up some laundry detergent and some softener, she was going to spend tomorrow morning at the laundry mat to get some things cleaned up. They didn't really wear all that much in clothing, the usual things, really, but since they rarely got out of the rig more than a couple of times a week, neither of them saw any reason to put on clean clothing daily.

While she was doing laundry the next morning, she took her mom's advice and picked up the local and larger city newspaper. It had been a lot harder than she thought it should have been to pick up actual papers, but she managed to find a couple. Mostly, it was the local stuff that she read, but other things were going on around town, too, that she was interested in. Like talk of the charity Tucker Charities.

It went on to tell how the Tucker family, along with the Fosters, had set up the charity to help people get back on their feet. Not just individuals but also companies that wanted to expand and or start up. Like the distribution center that she was going to be working for.

It was going to hire as many as six hundred people. All the work on the building was done by locals when it could be done, and once it was up to full capacity, including truckers like herself, there would be over a thousand new jobs. She wholly believed in the trickle-down theory in that if there were that many jobs, people from all other walks of life would benefit from it as well, like restaurants and especially schools. Her mom came into the laundry mat just as she was putting the last load in the dryer and showed her the haircut she'd gotten.

"I nearly fell asleep while she was washing my hair. It's nice to be pampered a bit, don't you think?" She told her mom that she didn't care for people touching her. "Yes, I remember that. You were always an odd man out. But I love you, and that's all that matters."

Her mom took the papers with her and said she'd be in the rig. As she was taking out her pants from the dryer, she noticed that there wasn't much going on in the place. Not that she knew all that much about laundry mats, she just thought that there would be more people in the place on a Thursday morning.

It took her two trips to get her things out to the rig, and by the time they'd gotten things put away and the things hung up that didn't go in the dryer, they were ready for some dinner. Ordering a pizza sounded good to her, but her mom wanted to sit somewhere that was larger than a table. In the shopping center where they were, two shops served pizza, and they decided on which one to go to after flipping a coin. If only life were that easy, as just a flip of a quarter could make the decision for life's little things.

"I'm stuffed." Emma looked around the room and noticed a man at the counter talking to the cashier. She wondered if he had wanted something to eat and didn't have the money when he turned suddenly and looked at her. She didn't move. There was something so very strange about the look he was giving her. "Mom, it's time we get back."

They were gathering up their things when the man came to their table. He didn't say anything but continued to stare at her. Finally, having had enough, she shoved him hard enough for him to hit the floor and stepped around him. Just as she was taking a step toward the door, he grabbed her leg and had her falling on her ass.

Turning around, she grabbed him by the arm and twisted. The sound of something snapping in his arm didn't make her feel any better, but she was free of him and stood up. Whatever was wrong with the man, she wanted nothing to do with him. As she was getting up, he came at her again, this time with a knife in his hand that had been on their table.

"Back off." She didn't want to have to pull out her gun, but her mom had no such trouble. Putting it to the back of his head, telling him to drop the knife, she was able to limp her way away from him.

Whatever was going on in the man's head, she didn't want to hang around and find out. As it was now, she was beginning to feel the pain of being tossed around and didn't much care for it.

Mom had the man on the floor with his hands behind his head when the police arrived. While she didn't know what his problem had been with her, he was pissed off enough for the police to take him away almost as soon as they arrived. Sitting down hard on the chair that had been right behind her, she felt something warm and wet running down the back of her head. Turning to look at her mom, she yelled at the girl behind the counter to call an ambulance. That was the last thing she remembered as the floor simply came up from beneath her feet and slapped her out. Christ, all she'd wanted was a few slices of hot pizza, and now she was going to have to explain why she wasn't going to be able to have dinner with her new bosses.

~*~

"They didn't say what the man was going to do to her. Please don't ask me that again, Denver. I might have to wrestle with you a bit before we get to the hospital." He laughed, and Bailee glared at him. "I'm serious. Her mother said that the man just came at them—well, Emma, at least, and knocked her around. If not for her being armed, there is no telling what might have happened to her. Did you know that Emma's mom was a former cop? That's good to know."

"I didn't know, no. But I'm glad for it." They were pulling into the emergency department parking lot an hour after hearing from Charlotte Holden. "I'm so glad that she called us. It's a shame that this happened, but I'm sure that we can get to the bottom of this soon."

"I wouldn't be so sure. He seemed sort of deranged, according to Charlotte. I'm betting that he saw her as a target or something and was going to simply rob her." Denver asked why he'd pick her. "I don't know. Perhaps because she's beautiful. Also, being a redhead makes me think that he believes all those stories about redheads being magical or something. I've even heard that some people think that they're evil and in league with the devil himself."

"I'd heard that too." They were shown to the room where Emma was, but the room was empty of a bed when they arrived. Ms. Holden was there, sitting on one of the chairs, crying. It was her that got the woman to stop crying and to tell her what was going on.

"The man had a picture on him that showed a red-headed woman who sort of looked like Emma. She had fuller lips than my daughter and seemed to be a bit heavier. But he thought that she was the woman at the welfare office who had taken his kids away from him. He was set to kill her so that he'd not have to face her in court. If he acts like that around his children, I'm glad they were taken from him. The man was set to kill my little girl." Bailee was sorry that it had come to this, but she told the other woman that she was glad that she remembered to call them. "That was Emma. She woke up a couple of times and told me to call you guys to explain why we might not make it to your house tomorrow night. We were having such a good day, too, when the man attacked us. The man who runs the shop we were in seemed to not understand me telling him to get the police until I had to smack him a good one. I hated to do it, but he was just standing there while Emma was bleeding on the floor."

"I would have been terrified if that had happened to me. Especially with it being my child." Denver asked where Emma was. "Oh yes, I should have asked that first thing. I'm sorry."

"It's fine. She was taken for a CAT scan of her head and neck. They haven't put any stitches in her yet. I think they were waiting for the tests to come back. I'm going to have to call someone to get the rig taken care of. The shopping center has a strict rule about leaving rigs on their lot overnight."

"I'll make a couple of phone calls, and it will be all right. Once we figure out what's going on here, I'll have someone drive it to our house, so you don't have to worry about it." Charlotte thanked them both. "Do you need anything, ma'am?"

"Just my girl to be all right." Bailee sat with her while Denver went to make the phone calls. It really wasn't that big of a deal to have it moved, but there was no point in leaving it out there to be vandalized. "I just wish we'd have eaten in the rig if it was going to cause all that much trouble."

Before she could say anything, Emma was brought into the room. She looked a little out of it, and the nurse explained that the doctor had said she could have something for the pain. Whatever it was, it looked like it was doing the trick for her.

"They're going to keep her overnight. Just to make sure that she's here to get some meds when she needs them." Bailee wondered what would have happened to her if they were to have released her since she and her mom both lived in their rig. She was going to make arrangements to have Charlotte stay with them and Emma when she got out of the hospital. It was the only way that they were going to get some rest, she thought. "Once the doctor looks over the scans, then we'll come in and put some stitches in her head. It's a good-sized cut, but shouldn't put her down for very long."

After explaining that she was a redhead and would need a bit more to knock her out, the nurse laughed and said that the doctor had a red-headed wife and knew how that was true. After she left, Charlotte went to the bed and held onto Emma's hand. Bailee felt her eyes fill with tears. After so many things going on with mothers lately, it was nice to see a family get along so well.

"Emma is my step-daughter. When her father met me, she was about two years old at the time. We dated for a while, and Emma and I became close to each other. Then, when her dad died suddenly, we were all each other had." She told her she was sorry. "I am as well. We didn't have a lot of time together, Frank and I, but we certainly loved this little girl. She's done so much for me that I don't know that I would have made it without her bullying me all the time. In a good way, you understand."

"Yes, of course. She told me how you bullied her at times as well. The two of you are good together." She said that they had to be because they were in cramped quarters all the time. "Yes, I can see how that would make a difference in a relationship. I don't know that I could have been in a rig for as long as the two of you have been."

"Like I said, it was for the best." Charlotte looked at Emma. "We, the two of us, have sold off everything that we owned to make this work for us. I wanted to see the country, and she wanted to drive so that she was her own boss. I have no idea how much longer she plans to do this, but I've never been so proud of anyone as I am of her. We have a bit of a savings account thanks to her, and we're doing something that very few mothers and daughters get to do with each other."

"I would imagine that you two are the exception to the rule about families getting along so well. Taylor, you'll meet her later. She's having issues with her mom right now. I heard from the courthouse that she's been arrested for threatening a sitting judge, along with a few other things that are going to get her jail time. Now that woman is a nutball." The two of them talked for a while, waiting for someone to come in and talk to them. Denver came back to tell them that the rig had been taken care of, and she could tell that Charlotte was relieved about that. She had looked it up earlier and couldn't believe the cost of a simple rig. And theirs had extra stuff in it for them to live.

It was nearly midnight when they admitted Emma. She didn't want to stay, but her mom said she'd feel better if she had. That was when she told them that their house was open for them and that they'd be proud to have them staying with them until she felt better. She had a feeling that the only reason Emma agreed was because her mom did so quickly. It was lovely to see such a bond between two people like she was.

After setting up Charlotte in one of the guest rooms, she and Denver went to bed, too. Tomorrow was going to be a long day as they had meetings all day with different vendors that wanted to come to the town. She was excited and scared at the same time. So many people were depending on them for new jobs and businesses coming in that it made her slightly nervous, too.

The next morning, Charlotte heard from Emma about when she was going to be discharged. The rig had been brought to the house, and she was happy to see that Charlotte was able to get herself some clean clothing. It was wonderful, too, that she got to see a first-hand look at the inside of the little home they'd been living in for the past five years.

"I don't think that I could have done it." Bailee thought about some of the magic that was in the family and wondered if they could tweak the rig a bit so that they had a lot more room. That was a question for later, she thought. She wanted to make sure that everything else turned out fine for the two women before the center was finished.

Several hours after having her breakfast, Bailee was ready to face the meetings that she had set up. Off and on, she would check on Emma, but for the most part, she was glad to be getting these meetings done with. She'd know better than to have them all on the same day again. It was trying for her to keep straight what each meeting was about. She felt like she was in a tennis match with things going back and forth.

However, at the end of the day, it was a great accomplishment to know that seven more businesses were coming to town that would hire two hundred people. Next week, they were going to do the groundbreaking for the parts place for wine barrels being made right here in their little town.

Dever was picking up something for dinner as they both had had a fulfilling day. Emma was in the living room, relaxing, and her mom was on the phone with someone. Once she left the room, Bailee asked her how she was doing. She could tell that she was in a bit of pain, but she said it was nice to be settled someplace other than a hospital bed.

"I would imagine. And something bigger than the bed that you two share." She said that there was that as well. "I'm hoping that you guys live close enough that we can get together sometimes. I fell in love with your mom, and she's having a good time house-hunting with the realtor."

"She's going to be spending the most time in the place, so it might as well be her who finds us something. I think she's finished with traveling now and wants to settle in one place." She nodded and then said that she'd spoken to her a bit. "Not that I'd turn her down if she wanted to go with me at times. Being home at night has been the most appealing thing you've offered us. Mom wants to put in a little garden and have a place where she can sit and read. I'm betting that we won't even own a television set when we get someplace. We've enjoyed the peace and quiet for too long for us to go back to wanting all that noise again.

"I can understand that as well. I was going to ask you, do you still feel up to having dinner with us all tomorrow night? I don't want to make you do anything that you don't want to do." She said other than a pounding headache, she felt pretty good. "Good. I was going to cancel if you thought you couldn't do it. I can't wait to get this project, along with a few more, started. It's going to be so good for the area."

There was more to it than that, but she didn't mention it just yet. Bailee was thinking that it would be wonderful if it turned out that Emma was one of the others' mates. However, since she wanted it to happen, it wouldn't. But time would tell, she supposed. Tomorrow was going to be another long and scary day with all the meetings that she had coming up.

~*~

He couldn't help but marvel at the sea this time of the year. Colby had finally gotten his first of four ships that he wanted, and he couldn't be happier with the way things had turned out. The LouCinda, named in honor of his grandma, was booked up until the first of February. The other three ships would come as he could afford them. And from the way things were looking, it wouldn't be that long of a wait.

The two that were going to really test his abilities

were the first one in a week that had five fishermen and the second one that was carrying eight. His brother Jack was going to help him out with the food and join him on the boat for a few days. It would be like old times.

Hanging out with family had always been his favorite thing to do. Especially when there were only a couple of them to do it with. Having nine brothers and sisters had made alone time nearly nonexistent growing up, so he was going to take it when he could get it. He'd have Jack all to himself for a few days, and they'd work on the ship together and then play around at night. He was glad that his new wife, Taylor, was all for it. He loved all his family, including the ones that had come to them through mates.

"Mr. Tucker? There's a landline call for you in the cabin." He and the crew that he'd hired were putting the finishing touches on the Lou to be ready in the event that someone wanted to go out today or tomorrow. Going into the living area, he picked up the phone and answered it.

"My name is David Sledge. I want to book your boat for the next three days." For whatever reason, Colby's lion wrapped around him as if to warn him of danger. "It'll only be for the three days, and I'm willing to pay double your rental fee if you could just let me and my crew have the boat for that amount of time."

"I'm sorry, I don't rent out my time like that." He said it would only be for three days. "I heard you, Mr. Sledge, but I'm not in the habit of renting out something without my being on the ship as well. It's not the way that I do business." He said that he'd rent the boat, but what about if it was just himself, but with his own crew that went out. "Again, I don't work like that. I'm sorry. You'll have to keep looking. To be honest, Mr. Sledge, I don't know that there is anyone who rents out a boat without her captain and crew."

"You're just starting out, Mr. Tucker. How can you have those kinds of rules when you've not even taken out your first group?" Again, his lion wrapped tighter around him. The man knew that he was new and that was why he'd thought to get him to do what he wanted. "I mean, can you really turn down something like double your fees at this stage of the game? It's just for three days. Two and a half if you'd like. Come on, now. I'll triple your fees, and neither of us will be out much of anything."

"I said that I'm not going to rent out my boat to you, Mr. Sledge. Now, if there is nothing else, I've things to do." The man growled low, and that was when he realized that he might be in just a little bit of trouble here. Reaching out for Parker Foster, the grand witch of all witches. *"I'm in trouble here. Big time, I think."*

"The phone call?" He told her that was it, and she told him not to hang up. He knew that one of the Fosters, he was too nervous to remember their name, could touch a phone and know just who was calling and where they were. Today, he just wanted not to be killed. Even if he couldn't, he didn't want to be hurt either. She told him that she had it.

"Listen here, buddy. You're going to rent me your boat, and you're not going to have one little bit of — Christ." When the line went dead, he gripped it harder to his face and sat down. If not for the chair being just behind him, Colby wasn't sure what he might have done. Landed on the floor for sure.

"I have it taken care of, Colby, my friend." He thanked her and asked what he needed to do now. *"Just hang up the phone. He's not going to bother you again. This I promise you."* That sounded scary to him. Very much so. So, doing as she said, still a little weak-kneed to do any walking, Colby sat at the desk and waited for her to come to him. He figured that she would, just to explain a little of what happened, but he wasn't even sure he wanted any information right now. Just as he was getting up to do the rest of the work on the boat, Parker appeared in the room with him.

"You were smart to call someone to help you." He asked her if he wanted him to dump a body. "Smart man. Yes, that's exactly what he wanted from you. Mr. Sledge had two, as a matter of fact, that he needed to get rid of quickly. You're a smart man."

"I'm a terrified one, is what I am." She laughed, and so did he. "As soon as he wanted to rent my boat without my crew, it scared me enough to know that I was in over my head. Will that happen a lot, do you think? That someone will think they can just rent my boat for nefarious things?"

"Yes. You're new to the area, and they figure that you have no experience with dealing with that sort of pushy person and that you'd cave when he got aggressive with you. Or that you're so desperate for money that you'll do just about anything to get a few bucks to keep you going. I'm going to make it so that you won't have that problem again. When men of his caliber are looking for a way to get out of a sticky situation call, they won't see your number anywhere." He thanked her. "You're so very welcome. Also, if something happens while you're out on a fishing trip, I'm going to give you a faerie to help. She'll be able to keep you apprised of anything that is going on from now on."

After Parker left, he felt a bit better. He'd even remembered to ask her about the trips that he had booked, and she told him he'd be just fine. Deciding that he needed to have some things on the boat to keep him and his crew safe, Colby got online and looked at things that they could use. He never thought of how far out in the water he would be with perfect strangers.

"*I have a couple of questions for you.*" He smiled when Jack contacted him. "*Do you have a menu that they can choose from? Like you know, lunch is sandwiches. Dinner will be three or four courses. Anything like that?*"

"*No. Though I think that sandwiches for lunch would be perfect. They can still enjoy fishing while eating. And smaller bags of chips to hold onto.*" They talked about having things easier to eat than what he'd have in his restaurant, and then things to have for dinner. "*If the crew catches some of the fish, will you be able to serve those up as well?*"

It was great to be able to bounce ideas off of Jack, too. He was a smart person to go to when he had questions about food and serving things to his guests. The one thing that he'd been sure to go over with him was a drinks menu. While there weren't going to be any drinks on his boat that he provided, a person could bring some of their own, so long as they signed a waiver saying that they were responsible for themselves if something were to go wrong when renting the crew and boat out. Also, he would provide the fishing gear for the trip. Again, so long as they signed a waiver if they were to bring their own, they were solely responsible for it.

There were other things that they discussed while talking, and when he realized it was coming up on six, Colby said that he had a date and needed to get ready for it. Of course, that got his brother to teasing him, and when he closed the connection, he was still smiling.

He knew this woman wasn't his mate. Colby had been out with her before. They were just fuck buddies. Each of them knew that nothing could ever be more than it was at that moment. Still, she was fun to have on his arm when he wanted a nice dinner and perhaps a play to go and see. No attachments were his favorite way to date.

Picking up Olivia at seven, they were headed to the restaurant when she told him about her job. She was a beat cop and enjoyed her job a great deal. There had been a murder-suicide happening today, and she was telling him how they'd found two frozen bodies in the place after the police were called. Colby nearly ran off the road when she mentioned frozen bodies.

"Are you all right?" He nodded, afraid that he might confess to something that he didn't have anything to do with. "You looked a little frightened there for a moment. Did you hear about it down at the docks?"

"No, I didn't hear about it. The radio was on. Maybe

I heard something about it then. You know how much Randy loves to have his music blaring." She laughed and said she wondered if he could hear very well, he liked it so loud. "So there was a man who killed someone, and you found the bodies in the freezer?"

"Something like that. The guy was a big-time thug that we've been trying to get for a few years. When the call came in about hearing gunshots, they sent someone to his residence and found four bodies on the front steps. In the house, they could see this guy named Archer sitting at his desk with a self-inflicted gunshot wound to his head. It looked like he'd shot the other four men, then himself. He actually left a note on his desk telling the police where to find the other two bodies. As you can imagine, it's been a day at work with this call."

Olivia trusted him as much as he did her. However, he thought that his trust of late was a little less than she was to him. Since the call today, he'd been jumpy, too, not wanting to tell anyone what he was feeling or going through. Colby was sure that even if the murder-suicide hadn't happened that way, that was the way everyone on the scene was going to see it. Parker would make sure of it.

After dinner, the two of them decided to go see a movie. It was still light out enough that they figured they'd walk to the theater and enjoy some popcorn as well. He couldn't believe how much it cost to just see a movie, but he was willing to pay it for a night of good conversation and fun. Colby didn't realize how much he needed this night, just as he was dropping Olivia off at her place. She said it was a bad night for him to stay over, and he found that he was all right with that. He wanted a good night's sleep, and being at home would pretty much guarantee that.

At three-thirty, his phone woke him up. It took him three tries to get the person on the other end of the line to stop talking long enough that he could figure out what was going on. It wasn't until he was sitting on the side of the bed, a faerie with him, that he understood that he needed to go and rescue someone. From where he wasn't that caught up yet, but he'd do it for the family.

"She's powerful upset." He told Crumble that he would be too if he'd been arrested. "Not Arrested, sir, but she's a witness to a death."

"Oh, I thought that she was in jail. Didn't you tell me that she was in jail?" Crumble explained again, he thought it was the fourth time, that while the woman was at the jail, she hadn't been arrested. Just a witness to a murdered human. Thinking he'd finally gotten it figured out, he drove them both to the police station and asked for Officer Colrain, who had been in charge when Crumble had been there.

"Is she your master?" While he hated that word, he knew that it was the only one that the little faerie would understand when talking about the person he was supposed to be looking after.

"Nay, she is my friend's master. Darling was off tonight, and I was with her. I didn't see anything. She kindly kept me away from the murderer. But she asked me to get one of the Tuckers, and you were the closest one that I knew to her." He was there because he was a Tucker and close. Better, he supposed, than being the one dead, he shivered. "I don't usually go out on trips like this one, but Darling's wife just had them a baby, and he wanted to be there with her. Emma, the master, understood and said it was fine by her to have another in his place. She's very nice, Ms. Emma. The others, your family, has taken her under their armpits and want her to keep safe."

"It's wing, not armpits." Crumble looked confused and said that humans didn't have wings. Letting it go, Colby changed the subject. "So why am I here if she's not in trouble? I'm assuming that she had some kind of part in the accident?"

"Nay, she had nothing to do with it. Because of her magical truck, she stopped in time to not do more damage. She is very lucky, the officer said, in that she didn't muck up—I don't know what that means—any more than it already is. It was three cars that slammed into one another."

Colby was getting more and more information and understanding less and less. He didn't have a faerie around all that often, but when he did, he knew them to be confusing and a little aggravating. It was why he had opted not to have one around him when he came here. He didn't want to have to spend all his time trying to figure out what was being said.

Finding the girl was easier than he thought it might be. She wasn't in a cell but in one of the offices of the large stationhouse. There was a blanket over her head, and he could see water stains on the back of the towel. Entering the room with her, Crumble said her name lightly so as to get her attention.

~*~

Emma looked at the man after asking Crumble if he was all right. She might well have done that several times over the last few hours, but she couldn't remember. She remembered a lot that had happened, but talking about the little person who might well have saved her life, she didn't remember.

"Crumble said that you were near an accident." She nodded and told him that it had happened right in front of her. "I'm sorry to hear that. He said that several people were killed when the crash happened."

"I didn't hit the car by an inch. By an inch." She tried to calm her voice down. "We were coming up on the light when this man in a red SUV leaned out of his car and shot the man in the car beside him. Just pulled out his gun and shot the man. I'm assuming in the head because the windshield splattered with blood the moment I heard the sound of the gunshot."

The man nodded, but she thought that he was humoring her. Looking at Crumble, he still had spots of blood on his...tunic? Dress? She didn't know, but it was on him. Pointing it out to him, he did a little body shake, and not only was he cleaned up, but he had on different colored clothing as well. Emma put her head down and closed her eyes.

"The police said that it was nothing more than road rage. When one of the cars tried to pass the one with the shot victim, he was shot, too. Like the man wanted to be first in the race, and he was going to kill anyone who got in his way." Someone asked, she didn't know if it was Crumble or the man if she'd been shot at, and she nodded before speaking. "He turned the gun my way even though I'm at least six feet above him. All the bullet did was ricochet off the front of the rig and hit his car. That must have pissed him off more because he was coming at me to my door to, I guess, kill me too."

The door opened behind her, and she didn't bother looking. Someone had been coming into the room since she was brought in a few hours ago. When someone put their hand on her back, it was all she could do not to scream and cringe from the warmth. Every part of her was freaking out, and she didn't much care for it. Sitting up, she looked at the woman.

"I'm Bailee. We talked the other day." Nodding, she sat up higher in the chair she was in. "You're just fine, you know that, don't you? No harm came to you as I promised you and your mother."

"I should be dead." Nodding once, she sat down across from her, and that was when she realized that they were alone in the room. There was also a cup of what looked like tea in front of her with a few cookies on the plate. "That little guy. He snatched me back and did something to me to make sure I didn't die, didn't he?"

"Yes. Crumble is very good at his job of protecting people. You wouldn't have died, not from the shooting, but had the man been able to get you out of the truck before he was killed, he would have surely murdered you. He would have run over you with your truck and killed—" She put up her hand, and Bailee stopped talking. "You're all right, as I have said to you."

"It scared me. The way he looked, he was just going to do what he did without anyone stopping him." Emma looked at Bailee. "My mom, does she know that I was… whatever I was?"

"She is aware only that there was an accident that you were no part of, but only as a witness. Nothing more. I didn't think that it would do either of you any good for her to know everything right now." Emma thanked her. "I had no idea when you left yesterday that this would have happened. I only wanted to see how long it would be before you were to get to each of the stores along Taylor's routes. For returns, you see."

"I know that shit happens, but this was about as close as I've ever come to hitting anyone or even causing damage to anything since I've been driving." Bailee told her that was why they hired her. "Thank you. I'm assuming that I still have a job? I mean, why would you come all this way if I didn't…how did you get here so fast? Is it that magic stuff again?"

"Yes, the magic stuff." She knew that they had magic. Not that she wanted to believe it, but if she were to be in her rig right now, she could go to her bedroom and lie down on a nice king-sized bed. Get her things out of dressers or her closet and take a shower in her full-sized bathroom that was tucked into the little spaces that were there for her. There was even a fully operating kitchen with a table and two chairs she could sit at should she want to have lunch while not driving. "You've decided to believe me when I tell you that we're magical?"

"Honestly? I have no idea what I want to believe. The living room in my rig begs me to say I believe you, but in my head, there are just too many things that tell me that there is no such thing as magic." She eyed her hard. "No one has to shift to make sure I understand that there are lion shifters, either. I got that, too."

Bailee laughed, and she didn't find any humor in her. Not any of them. If not for the contract, she might well not have worked for them had she not already signed it. There was something extremely strange about all the Tuckers, and she wasn't entirely sure that any of them wasn't a little off their meds.

"Drink your tea, Emma. It'll make you feel better." She eyed the tea and then looked at Bailee when she laughed again. "I promise you there is nothing in it other than a bit of sugar. The cookies are just that. Cookies. Just have a few sips, and you'll see, you'll feel much better."

"The police are going to send me to the hospital. They're afraid that I've had a bit of trauma. They don't know that half of it. I feel like I've been put into a large rabbit hole and can't find my way out. You're not helping." She told her that she was trying her best. "Yeah? Well, it's not working. I don't even know...I'm freaked the fuck out right now."

"No, you're just still wondering how you can be alive when he shot you. He did, you know. Shot you twice in the head. But as you said, Crumble saved you, and you're going to be just fine. Nothing happened that you can explain to the police. You understand that, don't you?" She said that they'd lock her away. "More than likely just put you in the hospital for a few weeks, but we can't have that, now can we? You have a good job, and it keeps you from getting hurt. I told you several times that we take care of those that we love."

She was, in the end, taken to the hospital. The man who had come in with Crumble when she was at the police station was hanging around a lot. Twice, the nurse had to ask him to move so that she could do something for her, but other than that, he didn't say much. He did look like he was pissed off, but she had enough on her mind right now not to be fucking with a stranger.

At two in the morning, she was released to go home. Where that was from where she was, Emma didn't know, but she wanted a good night's sleep and some food in her belly before she started driving again. She knew that she could do it, even after the scare, because it was something that she needed to do. Her mom had found them a home that she loved.

Emma didn't really care for the house that her mom had found for them. It wasn't ugly or anything, but it was too big. Three bedrooms wasn't all that large, but after living in the rig for the past five years, it seemed huge to her. It was the yard that she loved, she told her mom, and she was already putting a garden in so that she could have some fresh veggies when she wanted them. Another perk was that she could park her rig in the driveway, and it would not be in the way of her mom's car, which she'd gotten.

Someone had parked her rig in the parking lot of the truck stop. She wasn't too far out that she couldn't get to it without going through a lot of darkness, but it was safe as far as she could see. No bullet holes or anything that she could see, either.

"Do you have an extra blanket?" she asked the man, whose name was Colby, if he needed a pillow, too, not having any idea why he'd need a blanket. "I'm going to stay out here in my car to make sure that you're all right."

"I'm fine. It's stupid for you to sleep in your car when you have a home somewhere around here." He told her he had a boat, too, that he could sleep in, but wanted to be close to her. "I don't want you to waste your time sleeping around here. I'm going to get into my rig, lock the door, sleep for about forty hours, and get up and start again."

"All right then." She tossed a pillow and a blanket at him. She was disappointed when he was able to catch them both, but went into her rig and decided to forget all about him. He was an idiot if he thought that she was going to invite him into her place, especially after what happened that evening.

The bed was cozy and warm. Large enough for her to stretch out in, too. After getting herself situated, she thought a little about what Bailee had told her about lion shifters. And when she'd not believed her, she had her husband shift into his and lay across her lap. Emma had nearly wet herself when he did that.

But he had been beautiful. Never being this close to a large lion, she was told that because he was the leader of a leap, he was larger than his brothers, even the older one. His mane was wonderfully soft, and his fur along his face and nose wasn't anything like she thought it would be. The entire experience with him had been telling and a lot nerve-wracking.

Waking at some time in the middle of the morning, she could hear voices and didn't bother with getting up. It was Crumble, and he was talking to one of his friends, she supposed. The little man had saved her life. The very least that she could do was to allow him to have company when he wanted it. Rolling to her side again, enjoying the comforts of her rig, Emma closed her eyes and went right back to sleep.

At noon, her alarm clock buzzed, and she got up. It still boggled her mind that she had enough room in her rig to have a stand-up shower along with all the other things. Washing her hair twice, she was ready to face the day and to see how many more miles she could get under her belt before she wasn't allowed to drive again.

"Hi." She looked at the man before it occurred to her that it was the guy who had wanted to sleep out in his car. Not that she would have allowed him to sleep in her rig, but she did let him come into her space when he told her that he'd gotten coffee and donuts. "I got a variety because I didn't know what kind you'd eat."

"They're donuts. What's not to like about them?" She did get herself a glass of juice, not caring for coffee at all. When she was settled into her seat across from the man, she finally remembered his name. "Colby Tucker. Crumble got you when I asked him to get one of the Tuckers. I guess I could have handled it myself, but I was freaked a little out."

"You were a lot freaked out, not that I blame you. It was a close call for you. I'm glad that you're all right." She nodded, finishing off her second donut in favor of conversation. "I was wondering if I could follow you to your next stop. Taylor suggested it, telling me that you might need a second pair of hands when you get to the last stop. I guess you're picking up bags for the grocery stores."

"Im not sure what I'm supposed to do with them. I thought I was bringing them back to the warehouse." Colby explained to her that they were going to break them down so that no one store would have too many to deal with. "I guess that makes sense. Yeah, I suppose it's all right if you follow me. Or you can just ride in the rig with me. I'm used to having my mom around, so you being there all the time won't be too bad."

"Gee, thanks." She finished up her breakfast and told him that she had to get some supplies. As soon as she got out of the rig, he followed her. Whatever floated his boat, she supposed. But she wasn't going to allow him to bother her too much. She really did have a lot to do today.

Chapter 1

Taylor was spending the day with her grandma and Jack. Her mother's trial was going on, and as soon as she was given a date for her sentencing, she was going to have herself a little party and enjoy her mother being out of her life for a bit. She'd been driving her crazy since they'd moved in with her grandma and Jack in the family home. Well, it had been all her life, but it had been especially hard since she'd moved in with her husband and Grandma.

She supposed that her mother had been getting on her last nerve for some time now. It had been a long time in coming, this separation from her mother and her demands. And now that it was nearly over, she couldn't help but feel like she'd been given amnesty in the form of not having to put up with her anymore. And she'd decided that her mother's demands had more to do with her than Taylor anyway. At least that's the way she felt about it.

Gilda Jane had always been selfish about her time. Taylor was to be at her beck and call all the time, or she'd throw a fit about it. And it wasn't that she just wanted to hang out with her, but demanded, literally, all her attention on her. She still felt the hurt from her mother telling her that she'd never wanted her at all and was glad that she'd been able to care for all her needs when she got older. She actually said that everything was about her and nothing about Taylor.

Taylor hadn't been able to date, never marry, and she'd told her that if she'd had kids, she would make sure they never made it to term with her. That babies would demand all her attention, and her mother didn't want to be second in her life. She needed to be first and foremost in her mind at all times. Catering to her needs was all Taylor was good for; she'd told her as well.

It wasn't until she met Jack that she realized what she'd been missing in all her life. Someone for her to love and to be loved by, too. She and Jack had been married at the courthouse a few days prior to her mother getting arrested, and they'd been able to keep it a secret until she was put in jail for threatening the judge to kill him when she got out of jail. She had a feeling that was going to play a large part in her jail time, and she was not listening to anything anyone said about her. Again, it had to be all about her and nothing or no one else. Well, she supposed it was all about her now, but not in the way that she was craving.

At three, she heard from one of the jailers that her mother wanted to see her. She'd not go, of course. It would just be more of the same, and she couldn't take it anymore. Telling him to tell her mother that she was finished with her had felt good, though she knew it would be hard on the man who had called her. Her mother didn't ever like to be told no under any circumstances.

Just as they were sitting down to dinner that evening, she heard again from the jailer. Her mother had been sentenced to twenty-two years without any chance for parole. That suited her just fine, as she'd be well on her way to having the children that she never wanted her to have and so madly in love with Jack that things would be perfect for her. Not that it wasn't already, she reminded herself. With her mom behind bars, it had been wonderful to wake up every morning and not have to be dragged away from other things just to cater to her mother's needs.

"She wanted you to be locked up, too, so that she could keep an eye on you. Saying that you were 'fornicating with that man' and that you needed to be catering to her only, even if people were too stupid to realize that she should be first in everyone's thoughts." She asked him what she'd said when she was sentenced. "The woman actually said that she was going to get out and kill every one of the people in the courtroom. Then she did that thing where she looked around the room like she was memorizing everyone there. Scared a few people, too. I'm not going to lie, Missus, she scared me a bit, too, the way she kept staring at the lot of us."

"Perhaps she'll be too old to remember when she gets out." No she wouldn't, she thought to herself. Her mother would remember every bad deed that was put against her in the courtroom and beyond. It would be like her to remember their faces until she died, too. "We can only hope that she learns something while in prison. Even if it's only that the world doesn't revolve around her all the time."

She'd not learn that either, and she had a feeling that would be something that would get her killed, too. Taylor could well imagine her mother trying to get everyone to do her bidding until someone took exception to her and killed her where she stood. It wouldn't matter if they'd been told that she was like that. People didn't like doing everything that someone told them, no matter what was going on around them. Her mother wouldn't last a month, she didn't think, and it was hard for her to think of that as a bad thing. It hurt her heart that she was so over her mother that she would think of her being killed as a blessing.

After dinner, she and Jack stayed in the living room while Grandma went up to her bed. She was going on her cruise tomorrow, and it would be good for her. She and Jack would have the whole house to themselves, and they were planning on making a good go at getting in practice so that when she was ovulating, she could get pregnant on the first go at it. That's all she wanted was a baby of Jack's to make herself feel complete, now that she had a love of her life to be with.

As she was headed up to bed around midnight after spending a great deal of time on the phone with the stationhouse, she thought that she could sleep until the following morning, as she was so tired. With the opening of the new warehouse and the employee hiring, she had been busier than she'd ever been before. As it was now, she was short fifty or so employees and could use another dozen drivers like she had already hired. Christ, would there ever be enough hours in the day? She didn't think so at the moment.

"Did you get them situated?" She told Jack that she thought so. "It shows that they're eager to start work if they come in the night before you need them, doesn't it? I mean, I don't know what I would have done had that happened to me. I have a good crew right now, and if they showed up twelve hours before working, I'd just tell them to get a new job; waiting tables doesn't need that much dedication."

"Your staff loves you and would do that just to show you how much they care about you. It also doesn't hurt that they're making good money on tips, too. What did you tell me that you paid out last night in tips this morning? Wasn't it about four grand for six waitresses?" He said it was a little less than that, and he was happy for them. "I am as well. People always leave Jack's Place with a full belly and a big smile on their faces. That's what I love about the place, too. You wanted to serve comfort food, and people took that to heart. They love the place."

People really did, too. There hadn't been an open table since he'd opened, and there was usually a line out the door of people hoping to get a seat if they hurried through their meal for the next set up and table filled. It had been written up in some nice articles about the place, too, about how it's always busy but well worth the wait. One critic wrote their entire article on the mashed potatoes, telling how they were so fluffy and delicious that he compared them to his own grandmother's dishes she used to make when there was a family dinner. And she'd never been so proud of anyone as she was of Jack and Jack's Place.

Snuggling up with Jack, she closed her eyes. It was going to be a longer day tomorrow with getting things caught up, then it seemed like today had been. But she wouldn't trade anything for the world, as she loved being busy and seeing her idea come to fruition. With her businesses, she'd been able to create nearly five hundred new jobs for the city, and she was going to keep right on hiring until anyone who needed a job there was one there for them.

The next morning, she was asked to go and see her mom. She had no plans to visit her in prison, and the judge who had called her said that it might go a long way in paving the road to her own salvation. Not that he thought her mom was going to learn anything, she had been spouting off things like she was going to kill the judge as she was being dragged from the courtroom. But it might give her the closure that she might need down the road.

"I'll go and see her, but I'm not going to be nice about it. She didn't want me." He said he knew that was true, as she had said it a great many times during the trial. "Well, I don't know what sort of salvation it's going to give her when I'm not going to be locked up with her. I won't, will I be?"

"Oh no. That never entered the conversation on my part. No, you'll get to live out your life in relative quietness and happiness so long as she's away. Why her parents let her get to that point in her life is beyond me. Speaking of them, I have a letter here from them. It's been sent by their attorney out east. I don't know what it says, but I have a feeling that they're both gone now, and wished to let you know. That's my feeling on what's in here anyway. Come by my office when you're done with your mother, and we'll talk about things that are going to happen when she's in prison. There are rules she's going to have to follow that she's not going to like any more than she did when I told her you weren't going to be a part of her sentencing."

At nine in the morning, she was at the stationhouse seeing to her mother one more time before she was going to be carted away to prison. She made sure that she was dressed up; she didn't want her mom to ever forget that she was a businesswoman first and foremost. As soon as Mother was chained to the table and the floor, she asked her what she could want from her now.

"I want you to get me out of here." She said that she'd made her bed, now she had to lie in it. "They think I'm going to be doing housekeeping while away from you. You're going to have to tell them that I'm not doing that. It's beneath me. You should be in the cell with me because who is going to get me things when I need them? They also told me that I was going to have to eat my meals in the general population. I don't know what that means."

"You'll have to eat with all the other inmates like yourself in the dining room. There will be no special place for you to go when you want to take a crap, either, mother. Everything is right out there in the open with the prison you're going to, and that suits me just fine." She asked her what she was going to do to make her special at this place. "Nothing. I don't want to have another thing to do with you from now on. I hope you learn that not everything is about you."

"But everything needs to be about me. And you need to get up off your ass and make sure that everyone knows it, too. I have a list of things that you're to make sure I have. And don't think that you're going to get out of visiting me every day. I want you there from dawn until dusk so that I can keep an eye on you. Are you still living with that man? Jackass or whatever his name is?" She said that they were married and they were living as man and wife at the big house. "Where I should be, too. That's why this is all your fault, Taylor. If you'd have just let me live with you and that grandmother of yours, then none of this would have happened. See what you've done by not allowing me the same privileges that you have? I deserved to live in that house, too. You could have been giving me all that I needed without all this bother of that man. And now that you've married him, not that I believe that you have, you're going to continue to take your birth control so that there are no children. They'll be first in your life and I'll not—"

"I know, mother, you'll not have it. Well, I guess it sucks to be you because as soon as I can, I'm going to have a child and love it like you never did me. Also, I'm going to allow it to have a childhood like the one you denied me by being selfish and cruel and needing to be the center of attention all the time." She said that she liked being the center of attention, and she'd better not be having children. "I will because I want to love it…you know what? I'm done talking to you. If there is anything that you need, you're going to have to work for it. I'm finished wasting my breath on you."

"You'll do as I say because I'm your mother." She told her that she'd never been her mother, and that was just sad. "I gave birth to you even though I didn't want to.

Now you're stuck with me, and you're going to do what I want. I demand that you either get me out of this situation, which is all your fault, or you come and live at the prison with me so that I don't have to do the things that they want me to. I'm the center of your world, Taylor Ann, and it's about time you remember that. I'm all you have. And I'm all you'll ever have so long as I'm alive and well."

Standing up, she straightened her suit and picked up her purse. There was money in her bag that she had planned on setting up a fund for her mother when she got to prison. But that would be just one more thing that she'd hold over her. 'Why wasn't there enough in the account?' 'Make it so I have all your money so that I can be the center of attention when I spend it all on stupid shit just to spend your money.' It wouldn't be that way; she was sure of it, but it was something that her mother would need, and she was sick of catering to her every whim and leaving her heart open to being hurt again.

Leaving the little room, she decided that she was never going to see her mother either. She'd been tossing that around in her head as to coming to visit her once a month, but it would only be more of the same. Her mother making demands of her, and her heart hurting because of the way she'd been treated.

~*~

Colby had been on his boat for the last three days on a reservation to go fishing with five men. He hated to be away from Emma, but she was busy, too. He'd spoken to her about being mates, but she wasn't having any of it. To her, it was the same as a prison sentence, and she had a good job that she'd worked hard on as well as a new little house that her mom had picked out for them to live in.

"But you don't even care for the house. You told me that." She had told him that she didn't care for the house, even though she was planning to live there with her mother when she wasn't driving her rig. It was just that, a house. "I have to find us one that you'll like and want to live in. Even your mother can have a place in our house."

"I don't want you to buy a house simply because you think that I need one. I'm quite capable of buying my own home if it comes to that." She was being stubborn, and he was going crazy trying to figure out how to make her happy. "Besides, there will be nothing between us as I've said to you a million times while we were out on the road. I have a life, believe it or not, and it doesn't involve you or your mate business. Why would you want to strap your life with mine when you have everything you need already? Just leave me alone."

He couldn't do that. Not even when he was in the middle of the ocean with five strangers around him, he couldn't leave her alone. He'd been able to touch her, thankfully, or he'd not have a connection to her. That seemed to work now that they were mates and there was no need for the exchange of blood. Colby was glad; he didn't know what he'd do if he couldn't at least get into her mind to see what she was feeling at any given time. But she had Crumble with her too, and he promised to let him know if anything happened to her that he could help with. Like he knew anything about being a truck driver with a big rig. She more than likely knew more about his job than he did hers. He'd been talking about it with her when they were traveling together.

She'd allowed him to ride with her when she'd been doing a test run for the stores that Taylor had coming out of her warehouse. She drove the route that would hit all the stores that she had along the coast and stay for however long it would be for unloading. They figured two hours for that to happen at each store. It would be less time than it would have been with several trucks showing up several times a week, they had told him. Still, she could hit all the stores in one trip—provided that the loads weren't that heavy, and only have one stay overnight during the entire trip. If the loads were heavy, say at holiday times, then she might have to stay overnight as much as three times, but that would only be for a few weeks, not the entire season.

He'd not gotten this information from Emma but from his brother Jack. He had a wealth of information about the driving part of her job, and he appreciated it very much. He'd not realized when he was brought back from the trip that he'd only been the one talking about his job and she'd remained closed-mouth about her own part in the work she'd be doing.

"Mr. Colby, there's a phone call for you. It's a landline." He remembered the last time he'd had a landline call, and it made his belly churn up. The man had wanted him and none of his crew to go on a fishing trip in the middle of the ocean. But in reality, he'd wanted to dump a couple of bodies while out on the sea and more than likely kill him in the process. "It's your brother, Denver. He said to remind you that you're fine for some reason. You are fine, aren't you, sir?"

"I'm great. My brother just has a terrible sense of humor." He picked up the phone and asked his brother if everything was all right. Why did he have to talk to him on the phone? "I mean, I don't know how much these calls cost you, but they can't be cheap."

"I called because you're on speaker phone right now." He didn't understand that either. As he could get in contact with all his family at once through their links. "I have a gentleman here who would like to book one of your trips. He said that it would help him think about sealing the deal with him. *You're too busy to do it in the next three weeks. All right?*"

"*All right, I can be busy for you. Will you explain later?*" His brother said he would, but for now, he had to make things look good to the man in his office. "I'm sorry, Denver, but I'm booked solid for the next three or four weeks. Business has really picked up since word has gotten out about the last trip we made. Did I tell you that the fishermen caught their limit on the second day?"

"That's wonderful news. No, I'd not heard how well they'd done." Denver explained by way of their link that the man was trying to get them to pay for him to go out on a trip so he could think on whether or not he really needed the money to expand his business. "I guess my customer will have to think of something else to do his thinking with. I'll let you go and talk to you later."

"I'm sorry, Denver. I truly am." He told him that was all right, but he'd done good on selling the fact that he was too busy to take on another client right now. "I'll talk to you when we return. It's not for another couple of days, then I go right back out."

He really was booked solid for the next four weeks. Word had gotten around about how well the trip went and the amount of fish they'd been able to catch. He knew that had very little to do with himself and the crew, but the people who had rented his boat out had had such a good time that they had begged for another trip in the next month. It was his last opening before he got busy again with other fishermen.

Jack's restaurant had provided the meals for this trip. They had a choice of sandwiches for both lunch and dinner, and that was what they had opted for. There were other things that they could have had. Jack would have joined them on the boat to cook them some of their catch if they wanted, or to have a dinner provided by him of their choice. Breakfast was just donuts or bagels, another thing that they opted for, or there could be a large breakfast with Jack doing the cooking. He'd done it on other trips, and it was working out well for the two of them. People loved being catered to, particularly when they were paying a high price for it to happen.

Just as the men were sitting down to dinner on the ship, he reached out to Emma to see how she was doing. He didn't talk to her this way, only to check up on her. He was afraid that he'd startle her into having an accident sometime, and that would be bad for a great many people.

She was talking to someone when he touched her mind. It might have been someone at one of the docks that

she had to go to, or just Crumble her faerie. He had one
as well, and she was doing a good job of keeping him on
track with everything that was going on around his job,
too. Colby was glad that her faerie was supposed to keep
her from being harmed, and he'd done that already on her
first trip out for Taylor and Jack.

A man full of rage, road rage, actually had shot and
killed the man in front of her while they were driving. She
had only just been able to stop her rig from plowing into the
accident that it caused by one inch. When the man looked
up and saw Emma, he turned the gun on her. Firing twice
into her rig, he'd actually been able to hit her both times
with his gun going off and nearly killing Emma. If not for
Crumble being there, she would have died as a result. As
it was, she was terrified to have something else like that to
happen less and less as she traveled. He thought that was
the reason she was such a good driver. Something like that
had happened that made her more alert while she was out
on the road.

"What do you think you're doing?" Instead of startling
her, she did the same to him. He was at a loss to talk to her
when she snapped at him by way of the link that they'd
had. *"Crumble had to explain to me that it was you checking up
on me, that's why I feel like there is someone in my head all the
time. Do you know how distracting that is for me? Stop it. Or
just talk to me. That would be better than me worrying about
whether or not you're finding out something that will make me
have an accident."*

*"I didn't mean to distract you at all. I was just making
sure that you're all right."* She said she was until he started

searching her mind. *"I never searched your mind for anything but fear or pain. I didn't want you to be hurt."*

"I'm fine. I've been fine. I told you that I have my faerie with me, and unlike you, he's keeping his distance so that I can drive well." He told her that he was sorry. *"You should be. You're driving me insane. Just talk to me instead of lingering around in my head like a ghost might. Christ, I don't want to be your mate at all, and you're not helping your cause either."*

"I said I was sorry. I didn't mean to startle you." She said that he'd done it now and that she couldn't think beyond him stalking her. *"I'm not stalking you. I'm just making sure…you know you're difficult to have a conversation with sometimes. Are you always going to be biting and snapping at me when I just want to make sure that you're doing well?"*

"I might well be." She growled low, and it made his lion wrap tightly around him, keeping him safe from their mate. *"Listen, I have to concentrate on driving right now. I'm in heavy traffic, and talking to you right now is distracting me. Just let me talk to you when I'm ready. Which I'd not count on being anytime too soon. You're driving me insane with all this shit that is going on."*

Colby left her mind but wasn't happy about it. She could be kind of caustic when she wanted to be, and he wasn't sure what had caused that. Sure, he'd been in her mind, but she was his mate; what else was he supposed to do if she wouldn't let him make sure that she was all right all the time?

He didn't expect her to talk to him later, so when she did, he was startled once again. Not that he'd tell her that. She'd be picking the worst times to talk to him and have him messing up like he nearly did to her. There were things that he needed to concentrate on, and she would be there in his head at the worst times possible. Not that he'd turn her down. She was his mate after all.

"I'm better now. I have an hour unload time, so what did you want to talk to me about that was so important that you had to scare ten years off my life?" Instead of getting into that again with her, he told her how well the trip was going. And what he was doing at the moment. *"I can't imagine cutting up fish for people. I'm not a big fan of seafood anyway, but I love pasta. When my mom was riding with me, we'd have it at least twice a week. She did all the cooking while I did all the driving. It worked out well for us both."*

"Jack sometimes comes on trips with me. Especially ones that have five or more clients. The limit that I can carry is six; anything over that, and I can't take them out. It would overload the ship and make it hard to get around on the decking." She asked him if he was normally a rule follower. *"Yes, especially when people are depending on me to keep them safe. I would imagine that you have the same rules. That you won't do something that might make it unsafe for you to drive."*

"If I mess up, it might well cause a lot of damage to a lot of people. I could plow into a line of cars that would hypothetically kill all of them. I try not to think about that happening, or I might not get behind the wheel again. I have tonnage to stop when I have to, and it's no easy feat when I'm in the city." He told her that he didn't envy her job. *"I don't envy yours either. Being stuck in the middle of the ocean with strangers. I don't know how you do that without being terrified all the time."*

"I have a faerie with me, too, that does the same as

Crumble does for you. Her name is Buttercup, but she goes by Cup. She makes sure that I'm not going to get the worse of the worst kind of people on my ship when I'm out, either." She asked him if it was on purpose that her faerie was a male and his a female. *"Yes, it's to balance us out. Crumble is hundreds of years old, so he knows what to do in emergencies. While Cup is younger, not that much, but still younger, I have her to help me with chores around the ship, too. They love to be helpful, I've noticed."*

"Yes, so have I." They talked for the hour that she had, and he got the fish cleaned up for the men to take home with them when the trip was over. He usually cut himself once or twice with the sharp knife, but he didn't this time. He had a thought that it had a lot to do with the fact that he was relaxed, but he didn't know. She was calming his beast, too, for some reason.

Chapter 2

Emma made good time on her trip out today. She was home for dinner on time, and she loved that her mom seemed to be excited to see her. After telling each other how their days went, they settled into dinner and then cleaned up together. Mom did most of the work around the house as she was living there full-time, but she would help with the dishes when she ate with her.

"I've been to the library today. It's a really nice one that has a children's section that rivals most toy stores. I'm going to be volunteering there once or twice a week to read stories to the kids. Isn't that wonderful?" She told her mom that it was fantastic and hugged her when she seemed to need one. "Are you missing me even a little bit?"

"I miss you terribly. Especially at meal times. There isn't anyone to talk to." She said she could always call her. "I thought about that, too, and I might once in a while. But you need to get out more because this is what you wanted. I want you to be happy."

Emma remembered being told about Taylor's mom and how she wanted to be happy with her daughter all the time. She wanted her to make her the center of attention, no matter what was going on in her life. She couldn't live like that. It would drive her crazy to have to cater to someone all the time. That's why she and her mom got along so well; the two of them did their own thing.

Since she'd gotten up so early, Emma was ready for bed at nine-thirty. Dragging herself to the bedroom that was all hers, she realized that her mother had left it for her to decorate. She was fine with that. Having been able to put some final touches on the rig had been great since it was only her anymore, and it had given her ideas on what to do to her room at the house. She pulled up the shopping link and put several things in her cart before she was ready to call it a night.

Tomorrow was her day off, and she had things that she wanted to get finished in addition to her room. First thing she was going to do was to wash her rig. It had been needing a bath since her last long trip before working for Taylor Tucker.

Getting up early, something that she was used to doing anyway, she was out in the yard cleaning up the rig when the mailman came to the house. Mom had told her that he'd been coming around a lot and she wasn't sure how she felt about it. Leave it to her mom to be out of driving for a week and find a man who was sweet on her. She took the mail and had him moving along his way by telling him that her mom was busy. He looked so downtrodden that she wanted to get her mom and make her talk to him. Poor guy.

"You have a letter from the realtor about the house, I'm betting." She said that someone had finally made an offer on the house. "Great. Now, only if they can get financing, then that will be one more thing to get off our list of payments."

"I just paid the taxes last month, so we should be good for at least six months. Did I tell you that the electric bill came due, too, and I went ahead and paid it while I was writing checks out? I can't believe how much it costs to have an empty house with electricity. I don't remember it being that high when the three of us lived there." It had been her and her parents who lived there for five years. Then her dad had died one night, and that had left only the two of them. Since neither one of them wanted to live in the house anymore, it had been put on the market and hadn't sold yet. They were just waiting for the right buyer to come along and take it from them. She hoped that this was the one.

"It says here that they've put in an offer and that I accepted it. I did, by the way, before you get all defensive about it for me." It made them both laugh about how she would come to her mom's rescue even when it wasn't necessary. "I guess they're covering their asses with this one, or perhaps that's the way it's done now. I don't know, but I'd like for the house to be sold so we don't have to worry about it anymore." That was what she wanted as well. Not to have to worry about the house that they'd not lived in for over five years now. "And since it's paid off, everything we get out of it will be profit. I'll just use it to pay off this house, and we won't have to worry about this one either."

Not that they had to worry about that much. Since her father had died and left them well off with insurance money, it had been an easy life for the two of them. Even when she'd purchased her own rig, using the house as collateral, it hadn't been that much of a hardship to pay that off either. Now all they wanted to do was to get things squared away with her job, and things would look so much brighter for them.

The two of them had plans for dinner tonight. Mom wanted to try a new place in town, and she wanted something to eat that didn't involve using a microwave. She didn't want any bread either, as she'd been eating sandwiches a great deal over the last several days, and she was sick of them as well. As soon as they were seated, she nearly fell off her chair when Colby joined them.

"Your mom invited me to have dinner with you. I didn't think I was going to make it as the ship only just docked about two hours ago." He smiled at her mother before speaking again. "Thank you, Charlotte, for inviting me to have a meal with the two of you. I can't wait to try this place."

"Doesn't your brother own this place?" Emma wasn't happy that her mom didn't tell her about their unwanted guest, and she was going to take it out on him for being here. "Jack is the name of your brother who owns this place, isn't he?"

"Yes, he does, but he's been so busy that none of us have been able to get in to eat again." He picked up the menu and asked what they were having. "I know that the fried chicken is really good. I've had the mashed potatoes too."

As he went on about the menu and the things on it, she looked around the room. It was really busy, and she wondered how her mom had gotten a table. She was just about to ask her about it when Jack came out and hugged his brother and told her and her mom how glad he was to see them. She asked about the table.

"I keep one open in the event one of the family wants to come by and be seated. Since you work for us in a way, I wanted to make sure that you three were as welcome as I could make you. And dinner is on me." They all protested, but he was pretty insistent about it. "Just let me serve you guys my favorite and you'll have a good time."

The first thing that was brought out to them was the corn chowder. It was so good that she could have eaten enough for her dinner and been satisfied. There were also warm rolls that went with the table as well as an endless supply of iced tea that she and her mom dearly loved. Colby drank water all night, and she wondered why when there were other things to drink on the menu.

After the soup, which was really good, they had a nice creamy dressing on a bed of lettuce. There were other things in the bowl along with the lettuce, cucumbers, and thinly sliced boiled eggs. She loved the small tomato pieces as they seemed to absorb the dressing and make them taste better. Along with the homemade croutons, the salad was perfect as it could have been made.

The platter of chicken was next. And what a platter it was. There were at least nine pieces of crispy fried chicken that looked like the entire chicken had been brought to them. In addition to that, there were bowls of green beans with bits of bacon and onion in them, corn and mashed potatoes — her new favorite veggie — as well as gravy and corn bread slices. She was on her second piece of chicken when the platter of meat was refilled, and they brought out more cornbread as well as fresh glasses of tea. She was stuffed by the time they asked if they wanted desserts.

"I don't think I could eat another bite." Colby asked if there was any cherry pie left, and that's what he had. Mom ordered a dish of ice cream to clean her palate with, and she had a cup of hot tea. The perfect end to a wonderful dinner. Jack came out to see them again when their dirty plates were taken away. "That was the best meal I've had in weeks. Thank you so much for it. The chicken was to die for, I swear."

"It's the favorite of everyone that comes in and tries it. It's just our grannie's recipe that I'm using, and so is the gravy. I love real chicken gravy with chunks of chicken bits in it." They all agreed, and Jack hugged his brother again before hugging her and her mom. It was the perfect ending to a wonderful night, she thought. "Anytime you want to come in and have a comfort meal, just let me know. I really do have one table that rarely gets used unless it's family."

She was going to take him up on that, too. As they were leaving the restaurant, she realized that she was dead on her feet. Emma had gotten a great deal done today, being that it was her day off, and wasn't looking forward to driving tomorrow because she was so full tonight. However, she knew that she'd be on the road again in the morning with no ill effects from tonight. It was just good food that had filled her up. And she loved it.

"I was wondering if we could have some time to talk." She told Colby that she just wanted to go to bed and not have to be worried about mates tonight. "I wasn't going to mention that, but I'd like to offer you a ride on the boat tomorrow. We don't have anyone going out until the day after tomorrow, and I thought that you might enjoy it."

"I have to work." He nodded as if he knew she was going to say that. "I really do have to work. I get Tuesday off this week, then I'm off on Saturday again. Those are my only two days off unless they need me to fill in."

"Then maybe I can travel with you again. I really did enjoy that." She was tempted to say no; she had enough on her mind, but the thought of being alone tomorrow was just too much after spending some time with her mom and Colby. "I promise not to bother the radio again if you'll talk to me. We really do have a lot to talk about, and even if you don't want me as your mate, I have shared my magic with you, and we should at least talk about that."

"I don't have any magic." He said that she did and could prove it to her. When he told her to think of something she wanted to wear, she nearly passed out when her clothing changed to sweat pants and an old comfy t-shirt that she'd had forever. All she could do was stare at him open-mouthed until he closed her lips together by using his fingers. He didn't make fun of her either, which she was grateful for. "I didn't know that there was anything to do with magic. I mean, I'm getting a hard lesson in it with my rig. Parker, the grand witch, made it so that I have a lot more room in my rig, and I even have a full-sized shower with a king-sized bed, but I never thought that I'd have anything like that."

"I can do that as well. Change my clothing, I mean. It's usually the first bit of magic that we notice when we have a mate. There are other things as well. When you were handed the basket of teas with sugar, it didn't have the kind that you liked in it until you thought about it. Then all the tea was your favorite kind. I'll remember that for the future." She told him that she could get her own tea, thanks. "You're bristling again. Just go with the flow, please. I'm trying to be nice to you, but it's hard when you're biting at me again."

"I'm sorry. I feel like I'm in over my head with a lot of things lately. I don't want someone in my life who is going to order me to stop doing what I love. And I worked very hard for my license to drive the bigger trucks." He said that he knew that and would never presume to tell her what to do with her life. Only to make room for him in it. "I don't know, Colby. I have so much going on right now. We're trying to sell off our old house, and then there is the house we have now, in addition to me driving all the time. I just don't see us having any time for each other. And I won't give up my time to be with my mom to be with you."

"I'm not asking you to do anything like that, am I? I mean, not once did I say that you had to quit your job, either. You just assume that's going to happen and are fighting the battle without me ever doing anything to you about it." Colby looked so frustrated that she wanted to cry. It wasn't her fault that they were mates, and now he was pissed off at her. "Look, maybe we'd be better off staying apart for now. That way, you can think of something nice to say to me when I've done nothing wrong to you since I met you. I'll talk to you later."

When he walked away, she felt a little tenderness in her heart. Rubbing the area that was hurting, she felt tears roll down her cheeks. He'd just left her, and all she could think about was that she was going to miss something big if he didn't come back. Before she could call for him, her mom asked her if she was ready to go home. She looked like she was upset with her as well. Damn it, this wasn't her fault. None of it was.

Fighting with herself on the way home, she didn't talk much to her mom. She seemed to be all right with that, and when they got to the house, it didn't help her temper much when he mom got out of the car and walked to the house on her own. No one was playing fairly with her, and she didn't care for it. It was then that she realized that it was all on her, and she was the only one who was upset with herself. Her mom could have just been tired and wanted to go to bed. Stomping her way into the house, she was in her room when she heard her mom tell her good night. Christ, she needed to have her head examined. She was off her noodle.

~*~

Colby was so pissed off at himself for treating Emma the way that he had that he needed to cool off before going home. Instead of going to the condo where he was renting, he made his way to the boat to hang out there for a little while. He still had plenty to do, and clean up was his job when they came back from a trip.

He had the sheets in the washer when he started mopping the floor in the galley. Hardly anyone spent any time in there besides him and the staff, but the floor needed a good scrubbing. Tomorrow they were all off, and he was going to give the boat a once-over so that it would be ready for the next trip out. Pulling the sheets out of the washer and putting them in the dryer, he figured that he could get a good start on cleaning the rooms when he realized that he wanted to be with Emma instead of cleaning the boat and washing towels and sheets.

"What is wrong with you?" He never talked to himself before, not until he met Emma, but tonight, being all alone in the big boat, he knew that no one was around, so he could talk himself out of being upset with her while he was at it. "You're in love with her, that's what it is."

Was he in love with her? He'd never been in love before, but had seen his brothers when they had found their mates. He remembered seeing his grandparents loving one another in the kitchen once and had been so happy to know that they still had affection for each other after all this time. They were the most loving couple that he'd ever met. Nothing like his parents had been.

When he'd been just a little boy, his parents had dropped them off at their grandparents' house one Thanksgiving and hadn't returned for them. Just dropped off nine kids, all of them under the age of seventeen, one day, like they were nothing but rubbish they wanted to get rid of. And come to find out, that's just how they felt about them, too. Too many kids, and they blamed that on them. Like it was their fault that they'd had them.

Going to the house, hoping against hope that they'd be there just having some alone time, everything that they had ever owned, toys, clothing, and coats had been sold off so that they could have a 'fresh start' someplace that didn't involve them having to take care of all the kids anymore. Not that leaving them behind had netted them enough money for the lifestyle that they'd wanted. No, every few months or so, they'd be calling Grannie and begging for money. Like they had a right to do that after leaving two elderly people with all those mouths to feed, clothe, and take care of all the time.

Sitting at the galley table, he thought about how hard it must have been on his grandparents, too. Not only did they care for them and make sure they had plenty to eat, but when someone came along and needed a hand up, they were there for them as well. They'd also made sure that they were able to go to college when the time came. One of his brothers was an attorney, and two of them were doctors. They'd done all that for them without a word of hate toward their parents, too.

Colby decided that he was going to go and visit his grandparents tomorrow and tell them how much he loved them for what they'd done for them. He was also going to take them out to dinner so they'd not have to do anything about that meal, too. Hell, he should get everyone together sometime soon and see about getting together as a family around them. They were in their nineties right now, and he knew that they'd be around for a good deal longer, but he wasn't going to wait. He wanted to spend as much time with them as they would allow him to.

The beds were all made up, and the kitchen polished to a high shine when the sun was coming up. His plan had been to only clean a little tonight and spend the rest of the morning getting things squared away, like making the beds and sweeping the carpets. Just as he was heading out, one of his staff showed up to help him get it ready for the next trip, and he told her that he'd gotten it all done and was going home to take a nap. She seemed so excited to hear that he did a little dance on the way to his car. Next time he'd be getting help, he thought, and that would balance it out for the others, too.

Going by his condo, he took a long, hot shower and went to his bedroom. There was very little of anything personal in the place; he'd been spending most of his time getting the boat ready for going out. But he'd take care of that soon enough when he found himself a new home, one that he could grow into. He thought about asking Emma to go with him to look, but he wasn't going to bother her while she was out on the road. Besides, he was still a little upset with her and didn't want to seem like he was a sap just hanging onto her every word.

Getting up at noon, he was headed out the door at one in the afternoon. His grandparents didn't live all that far from where he was living, so instead of driving himself there, he instead walked. It was a beautiful afternoon today, and he wanted to take advantage of it as much as he could. As soon as he was in the house, he could tell that they'd missed him as much as he missed them. Grannie even got a little teary-eyed when he told her that they were going to dinner tonight, as he had missed them a great deal.

The rest of the afternoon was spent with him helping around the house. There was staff for them to use, but Grannie wanted to wash her own windows. Or she wanted them washed, and he was going to do it for her. Being up on the ladder for her, she told him how she'd been gardening a little and had too much food to put up without all the extra mouths to feed.

"I'll gladly take some of it home with me. I can cook a little, but I don't usually. It will be good for me to eat at home more." She asked him if he was enjoying himself. "I truly am. There is an ocean all around me when we're out, but it's the little things that I get to see that make it worthwhile being out there. A couple of days ago, while out, I saw an ocean liner out for a cruise. The people aboard her waved at us like we were something else. I've seen whale breaching. You can't imagine how wonderful that sight is, Grannie."

They talked about his job and the things that the two of them were doing as he finished up with the windows. Grannie and Grandda did not have to work; they were all sending them money to care for them every week, but they still did things around the neighborhood. Grandda was plowing up gardens for people who wanted to start one, and Grannie was giving lessons on the piano. Colby figured that was why they had lived so long, because they were so active all the time.

After he was able to fix the door that squeaked too much, they were getting ready for dinner. Colby knew too that his family had called the house, checking in on the couple, but as far as he knew, no one knew that he was there helping them around the place. It was like he'd had them all to himself and loved every second of it. At dinner, Grandda told him how the yard was being mowed by this kid who didn't do such a great job.

"I tried not paying him, but that brought his parents to the house. They were none too pleased that I wasn't going to pay him for a shoddy job, you know. When I told them how he'd missed large areas of the yard with the way he was rushing through it, the father told me just to pay him, or I'd be out of a person doing anything for me. So you know what I did?" Grandda was laughing, so he knew it was going to be good. "I showed him what an elderly lion looks like when they feel they've been taken advantage of by some humans. He didn't do a shoddy job anymore, nor did he complain about how my yard was too big for him to mow in one afternoon. Never heard a peep out of the parents again, either. I showed them, didn't I, Son?"

"You did at that." Sometimes he forgot he was a lion too. He'd been so busy that he'd forgotten to allow him to go on runs lately. "I tell you what, Grandda. I'm off tomorrow. I'll trim your hedges. I noticed they were getting a little high, and then go running on your property if you don't mind. I've not had much of a chance to get out of late, and being in the middle of the ocean doesn't leave much room to run around as one either."

"You do that. I might even go running with you for a bit. I've been sort of neglecting my old beast for some time, too. Other than the boy and showing off to him, I've not had a chance to get out since we moved here. And that's been several months." Colby asked Grannie if she wanted to go, too, and she turned them down. But to run with his grandda would be a rare treat that he would treasure for a long time. "We'll have us an evening of it, then have some dinner at the big house again. That'll be fun, won't it?"

"It'll be more than fun. It will be fantastic." The dinner was good and they enjoyed it a great deal. It was more the company than anything, and he was excited to have thought about doing this more often. His grandparents were special to him, and he wanted to spend as much time with them as he could. "I'll be over tomorrow, but I'll be gone for the next five days after that. Let's make up a time when we can meet up again and have some fun."

They both agreed with him that they wanted to do this more often, and he was happy too that they wanted to spend time with him. They even asked him if he wanted to spend the night in their home, and he readily agreed. It was just like old times, him under the roof of his grandparents with the warm blankets on the bed that had been made by Grannie and the bed made by Grandda. He had been making furniture since he was a child.

The next morning, he was up and working on the next project when Grannie called him to breakfast. Just like before, there was enough to feed them all, and he so loved her biscuits and gravy. He wondered what kind of food people had that lived around them and decided that it couldn't have been as good as what he was having. He was going to take some of the homemade jelly home with him so that he could have a snack once in a while and think of home.

All he could think about all day was how much fun he was going to have with his grandda. Once the projects that he'd been given were finished up, he and his grandda shifted and became their lions. It really hit him hard how old his grandda was looking, and it made him sad that they had been taking care of them for so long and now they were getting too old to do much more than sit around the house. But they kept busy, and that's what made them the best that there was in the way of family.

Chapter 3

Her return load wasn't all that much. Just a bunch of cardboard that would recycle. A lot of places were doing that now, and it saved a lot of trash in the dumps, as well as something new was made into the products. She even recycled in her rig, though on a much smaller scale.

She was ready for home. While she had a lot to do when she got there, the first thing that she wanted to do was have a nice meal with her mom. She'd been talking to her a lot through the chat application, but it wasn't the same. This time, she wanted to talk about how much profit the house made them when it sold and what she was going to do with it. They didn't have any large outstanding bills, but the house they had just purchased. Then her thoughts went to Colby.

He'd called her last night to tell her that he was going house hunting today and that he wanted to know if she'd come along with him. Emma's first thought was to tell him no, she didn't have anything to do with his getting a new home. But she'd been talking to a friend of hers who was a shifter too. He told her that if she didn't at least live with him or something along those lines, that he could go rogue. That's what wolves did when they lost their mates. And she wasn't going to be responsible for him doing anything that would cause trouble.

Emma had lunch plans with him today. After that, they were going to look at three houses that he'd picked out as well as see a realtor to see what sort of houses were on the market that she'd like to live in. He told her that the only thing that he wanted in the way of a house was a large eat-in kitchen, and she was fine with that. But she didn't want to have fifty bedrooms that he might expect her to fill someday with children.

She'd caught herself being snippy about him when he wasn't even around. And that bothered her. Emma wasn't a nasty person to other people, and she didn't know what it was about him that had her snipping all the time.

Pulling into the driveway at ten after ten, she was ready to call it a day. She didn't have any laundry to do, nor did she have to clean up the rig. It was in good shape thanks mostly to Crumble. Her mom met her at the front door to her house and hugged her. She felt like that was something that she'd been wanting for years instead of the few days that she'd been gone.

"I love you so much, Mom." She had to wipe at the tears that were falling down her cheeks. "I'm going to have to get used to you not riding with me. It gets lonely out there on the road without you around."

"I miss you around here, too. And I have all this room that I don't seem to know what to do with. Yesterday I went and bought myself a television, just a little one, so that I could have something that made noise around here. It's made a big difference." Emma told her about the date that she had with Colby. "He called here a few minutes ago to let me know that he was coming and if I wanted him to pick up anything from town. He's really a good man, honey. You should at least give him a bit of a chance with you."

"That's why I'm going with him to find a house for the three of us. You still think you might want a room at the house, right?" She said she was still getting used to the little one and that he would more than likely want something big. "I don't want anything big. I just want a couple of bedrooms, an office, and a place to park my rig. The rest can be on him."

"That's all someone could hope for, I suppose." Mom wasn't going to go with them as she thought that she might. She had things to do. Mom was making jelly from the fruits that she'd gotten at the store. Next year, she was going to put in a garden and have a couple of blueberry bushes put in so that she could have fresh year-round. It wasn't hard to do in the area where they were living. "I'm going to go to the library in the morning. I get to help the older patrons learn how to use a computer. I think that will be fun. Or not, I can't decide."

Colby pulled into their driveway a few minutes after they went into the house. She was glad to see that he didn't dress up too fancy; his jeans and polo shirt were perfect for the weather that they were having today. After talking to her mom for a few minutes, they were off to the first house. She only hoped that she could hold onto her temper, which seemed to be out of control of late, and have a good time with him.

The first house they looked at was perfect for her. There was a long, wide driveway that seemed to be double what she'd need to park her rig. The house had an eat-in kitchen, too, which she loved. However, when she was going through the bedrooms, something about the way that they were set up threw her off. It wasn't until Colby pointed it out to her that she realized that there was only one bathroom on the entire second floor and nothing in the master bedroom.

"That would make for a very crowded morning if your mom stayed with us. Not to mention, the bedrooms are so small. I bet nothing more than a full-sized bed would fit in them without dressers." She was happy that he didn't mention children, too. But he was right, it would be difficult to get any kind of bathing situation finished up with only one bathroom. "I'm not even sure that the dining room is big enough for much more than a four-top. Unless you don't plan on using that room."

"I would like to at the holidays. But you're right. Again. The rooms are just too small." Emma turned to Colby and looked at him. "I don't know what's wrong with me. It's like I'm antsy all the time. Like I'm crawling out of my skin."

All he did was put his hand on her shoulder. And it was as if he'd cured her of all the things that seemed to be wrong with her. Her body relaxed, and her mind seemed to just chill out. Putting her hand over his, she closed her eyes and moaned. It was the first time in weeks that she felt like a normal person. She asked him what he'd done.

"Nothing but centered you. Sometimes I need it as well. Just to touch from you to know that things are going to be all right." She asked him again what he'd done. "Nothing, I promise. All I did was give you comfort. That's the only thing that I can think of to call it. Comfort for the both of us. We've not been spending too much time together, so this is the only way to keep me from pulling you into my arms."

"I'm not ready for sex yet. I mean, I've been talking to a wolf friend of mine, and he was telling me some things that would happen now that we're mates." She asked him about the point of him going rogue. "He said that his kind will go mad if they can't have their mates around them and have to be put down."

"We don't have that. Lions are very laid back when it comes to mates. However, unlike lions in the wild, we only take one mate, and it's the forever kind of mates. I wouldn't anyway, but I can't lie to you, not even a small fib. If you ask me something, it's going to be the truth, so be prepared. Also, I won't have an affair. You're the only one for me for the rest of my life. I won't ever cheat on you either. You can take that to the bank." She asked him why that was. "I don't know, honestly. It could have something to do with the fact that we fall so hard in love with our mates that there isn't any room for anyone else. I know you don't want to hear this right now, as we're taking it slow, but I'm in love with you. I understand that it will take you time to get to know me, but I couldn't be more in love with you if I'd known you for a thousand years. And I'll love you more each day that we're together as well."

"Thank you. I think. Honestly, I don't know what to think. But I can now. Before you touched me, it was like I wanted to bite everyone's head off, and my skin felt like it was peeling off me." He said that he gets that way, too, when he can't talk to her. "I do feel better after I talk to you. I don't understand it, but I guess that's the way it should be. All right, let's go to the next house."

The second house was no better than the first one. The rooms were much too small for even the basics in a bedroom. There wasn't a dining room, and the eat-in kitchen was the only place to have a meal. Even that was too small for what she had in mind. When she felt herself getting overwhelmed, a new word for how she was feeling, she could just reach out and take his hand into hers, and she felt it all melt away.

The third house had potential. But it would take a lot of work to get it up to standards. Colby said it might be easier and cheaper to start fresh with a new build. She kind of liked that idea, too. As they went to the office of the realtor that was going to work with them, she saw a house for sale by owner. Pulling into the long drive, she didn't like the way that front porch was cluttered. Knowing that she'd not do it that way, she got out of the car and reached for Colby's hand. It was that or yell at the people for making such a mess of the first thing people would see when they came to visit.

"It's all fine." She nodded once at him and put a smile on her face to see the people coming out to greet them. "We can make it into anything we want."

She looked at the house without the clutter. And it was too. There were about a dozen chairs on the front porch, as well as about that many more baskets filled with flowers. While she had no qualms about having flowers on the deck area, there were just too many of them for her to be able to see what potential things had. There were places to sit on the decking, but it was just too crowded to enjoy it.

"We've only just put it on the market today. You're the first to see it." They were invited into the house, and it was much the same as the porch. Even the walls were so crowded with pictures in frames that they overlapped one another. The living room, the first room that you saw to your left when entering from the main hallway, looked like it had been a store for used furniture; there was so much in it. "We had to wait until we had it looking good before we invited anyone in."

The entire house was decorated with the same crowded motif. The kitchen was the most heavily crowded room with roosters, cows, and pigs all over the countertops and on the walls. She could see herself working in the room without all the décor, and she was happy about that. They must have spent a fortune on all the new things in the house to make it look homey to them. To her, it just looked like a train wreck, and she hated to think about that toward the people showing the house to them.

"How much acreage is there?" That, Emma thought, was a good question. She'd need to pull her rig someplace as the front of the house held no area where she could do that. After being told that it was about five acres, she thought that she could work with that, but it was the barn that was next to the house that caught her attention. It would be nice to be able to park her rig someplace other than out in the open, where it might devalue the property.

Emma was impressed with the price of the house. The couple older than them said that they wanted to sell it and move to Florida, where their children were. Why would anyone want to live there when they had all the warmth and wonderful weather that they had here was anybody's guess, but then she loved where she was from more than anything else about the state.

Leaving the house, she couldn't decide if it was someplace she wanted to live or not. There were a lot of things about it that they both loved, but she couldn't get over all the clutter. Like it was hiding something that—when Parker appeared in their back seat as they were preparing to leave, startled them both.

"The foundation is in poor shape." She nodded, not really having any idea what that meant. "The foundation is what holds the house above ground. This one is falling in, and the clutter, as you called it, was just a way for them to hide the cracks in the walls and floors. They hope that people will be so distracted by the amount of shit in the house to notice that the house is falling down on itself."

"Well, that's not right." She agreed with Colby. "No wonder it's not sold. I guess it's been close a couple of times, but the sale didn't go through. I'm assuming that someone did an inspection on the place and found what you said to be true."

"Pretty much. But in another five years, probably less, the house would be one earthquake away from falling into ruin." She didn't want to think about what would happen if anyone was living in the house when that happened. It would mean certain death if the house fell on someone. "You'd be right in saying that. However, you'll be happy to know that someone else, another witch, put a spell on the house that makes people feel uncomfortable in the house, and it never sells. You guys might well have felt that when you were looking around."

"I did." Colby looked at her. "Remember me telling you that the house felt like it was magical but not in a good way? That's what I was feeling."

"I couldn't get over the amount of shit that it cluttered around the entire house. It was like it was all a garage sale and they were making sure that there was something for everyone to buy." The three of them laughed about that, and it was funny to think that the place had been overdone to make sure no one could see the underlying problem. "Will they ever sell the place?"

"Doubtful. People are less trusting than they used to be, and in this case, it's a good thing." They all agreed and were on their way to the office when Parker told them that she'd given them both a bit of magic to be able to see behind the lies that people told about their homes. Parker continued with an idea. "I have about a dozen houses that are on the market right now by owner that you should have a look at. Not all of them, but enough that you can find a place. Did you know that the house right down the street from your brother Denver, is for sale? It'll be a good buy for anyone looking for a nice warm home."

"Should we just purchase it now?" Colby was joking, but she thought that if Parker recommended a house, they really should just buy it. "What's the address, and we'll go and see it?"

After getting the address, they made their way there, telling the realtor that they'd met her there. Even before they saw the house, she knew that it was going to be their home simply because she trusted the grand witch. She'd not steered her wrong so far. And had kept her from getting killed when there was the accident with her truck.

The house was a little larger than she had thought she'd want, but it ticked off all the things that she had wanted in a home. There was even a pool in the back yard and enough room for her to park her rig in the large metal barn in the side yard that was as beautiful as the house was. Inside, there wasn't any clutter, but a nice empty house where there was room for all kinds of their own things, and she loved it. As they were touring the kitchen, the realtor said that it had been upgraded sometime in the last year, and it looked it. She was in love with the entire home. And she couldn't wait to make it their own.

~*~

Colby got the loan for the house and even had saved up enough money for a sizable down payment on it so that they're payments weren't going to be much more than he was paying in rent toward his condo. He would have gone into debt more since Emma seemed to really like the house, just to have something that she could love. He'd not been kidding when he told her that he was in love with her. He felt his heart beating only because of her.

Since the house was empty and they were getting the loan, they could start to move in as soon as they wished. The people who had owned the house were so excited about the house selling so quickly that they offered to pay for a semi to move them. With Emma's help in knowing how to drive a semi already, it was going to be a breeze to get their things to the new house. Not that either of them had all that much in the first place. He had his bed and dresser, and that was about it. She hadn't anything but her bed, too, but she was planning on leaving that with her mom so she could have people over if she wanted. They didn't even have a dining room table to use.

Colby had to go out tomorrow morning on another fishing trip. His second mate, Charlie, was going to be manning the ship once it was out, so he could get better at running a trip. When he was able to afford more boats, he was going to have to have someone who could run trips, too, and was glad that his partner was ready to get the second part of his plan ready.

This way, he didn't have to do all the work either. Once he was trained, he'd be able to take out twice as many trips, and that would be great. The Tucker Foundation was going to help him with the second purchase, and he couldn't have been happier about that either.

When his cell phone rang, he always got a jolt of fear that someone was going to be calling to take over his trip to hide a body. Parker had taken care of that for him, but it was still hard for him to remember that he was safe when it rang. Answering the call, he was surprised that his grannie had called him.

"We've got some things going on around here, and I was wondering when you can come back out and give us a hand. Your grandda had purchased some new roses to put out, and we thought of you coming to help." He said that his next day off was in three days. "Perfect. The new soil will be arriving on Wednesday, so that will be timed just right. I'll make you dinner, and you can spend the night too if you wish."

"Yes, I'd love that." He was going to have to work around his schedule a little, but he wanted to help his grandparents. As soon as he told her that he'd seen her on Thursday, she simply hung up. It was just like her to do that, too. Once she was done with the conversation, she was finished with the call too. He loved that about her. Grandda did the same thing, only he'd say goodbye sometimes.

For the rest of the afternoon, he ordered supplies for the trip that was going out tomorrow. He would have to get Charlie to do it too, so that he knew what was needed or not, but for now, with the one boat, he was glad to be getting it done. As soon as he was finished with the order, he began looking over some of the things that they'd put on a list that they'd need for the house. When he got back from this trip, he hoped to have all that was needed shipped to them, and it would be one less thing to have to worry about.

"Colby, do you have a minute?" He told Candi, one of his workers for the trips that he always had time for her. "I'm pregnant. I didn't want it to happen right now, not with me getting a good job and all, but I have to think of my new addition."

"Are you quitting?" His mind raced to figure out what he was going to have to do to replace her tomorrow if she was quitting already. "I sure could use you tomorrow, but I understand if you have to leave now."

"I'm giving you a month's notice. That's plenty of time to get someone trained again, isn't it?" He said that he'd make it work. "I'm really sorry about this, but I don't know that I want to be huge pregnant while out on a fishing trip. I don't have morning sickness yet, but I'm sure with the swaying of the boat that it's going to be difficult to keep my soup down."

"I understand. I do. And I don't know that you'd be safe out there either. You're going to be a little clumsy, too, I'm betting. My sister was forever falling down when she was large with child with her two." Candi burst into tears, telling him how nice he was being to her. "I know what it's like to have someone having a child around me. My sisters both have them. We'll be all right. And if you ever need a job again, come and look me up. You've been a hell of a worker for us, and we're going to miss you."

When she left him, he got back to work on trying to figure out an ad so that he could put it in the paper that he was in need of some extra hands. He was also going to have the Tucker Foundation put it out there that he was going to be hiring three new people, hoping that at least one of them would work out as soon as possible. He didn't want to go through the process of hiring and training someone again, but it had to be done. Maybe he'd find that all three of his new people would work out and he'd keep them around for the new boat when it got it.

Right now, it was going to have to be on a delay because of being short-staffed. But he had no doubt that he'd get it finished up and working in his favor in no time.

He just needed to get people to come into the interview, past the drug and background check.

By ten that evening, he was headed home. He should have gotten out earlier, but every time he thought of leaving, something else would pop up. Mostly, it was calls from his family. They'd found out that he was helping the grandparents out, and they wanted a part of it too. Glad that they wanted to help, he was disappointed when Denver said he'd help with the roses, as he could be there when the soil arrived. He knew that all of them were going to help them out, and it would be a good thing. They'd spend some time with the grandparents and have a good time too.

Dragging his ass home, he was nearly there when he remembered that he didn't have any groceries in the house. Not even any milk so that he could have a bowl of cereal in the morning. Going back out seemed like too much trouble, and he decided that he'd grab something on the way to the docks. Christ, it had been a long day, and he still needed to take a shower and get his clothing ready to go out tomorrow.

Just as his phone was telling him that it was midnight, he was finally able to get into his bed. Setting the alarm for a good time for him to get up, he nearly sobbed when someone touched his mind. Didn't anyone have any schedule that they followed? Colby was happy when it was Emma.

"Sorry it's so late, but I had to ask you something. I know it's really late, but I have to go out tomorrow, and I was wondering when the next time you're off so that we can go

furniture shopping. No big deal if it's not soon. I know we both have jobs that will have to be worked around." He told her that it just so happened that he was off Thursday through Saturday. *"Great. I should be back tomorrow night, and I've asked to have those days off too. All right. We'll split the cost of the household things between us. I know we didn't talk about money, but I have a little bit. Not a great deal, but a bit."*

"I have money. As part of the foundation, I get a check each week for working there once or twice a week, and I've been banking it. Also, I have a nice-sized account from the trip funds that I can use for this." She said she was sorry again and told him she was glad that they could get together. *"Are you feeling any better about being overwhelmed? I know that since I get to talk to you often now, I'm feeling better too."*

"I do feel better. It's like things are settled, and I can move on with things that were bothering me before. Thanks for telling me about the touch thing." He said it was his pleasure, and she laughed. *"Sometimes it's all I can do not to pull off the side of the road and contact you, I'm stressing out. Did I tell you that Taylor has all the drivers she needs? That's why I can get those days off now. She's pretty excited about it, too."*

"She told me when I spoke to her today. Taylor said it was nice not having to rely on her wits to get the product to the stores, but with people like you working for her, she's not as stressed about it either. I'm assuming that Jack helps her with that stress." He felt his face heat up when he thought of the way his brother might be helping Taylor, and didn't know what to say to her. He was as embarrassed as he'd ever been. He decided to change the subject. *"We'll drive to one of the bigger cities to have a look around. There isn't much*

around here for furniture that we might like."

After deciding what time to meet up and who was driving, they closed the connection. It made his day not seem so overwhelming after talking to her, and he was glad that she'd contacted him. As he was getting ready for tomorrow by lying out his clothing, he thought of all the things that had been going on of late. He needed to slow down some or he was going to burn himself out. That was the reason they'd moved out here: to get more time to spend with family and to rest a bit more. He didn't want to fuck that up by being overworked when things were just beginning to look up for him.

Smiling to himself, he got into bed. Tomorrow was going to be a better day, and he couldn't wait to get started on it. And even if it was hectic, he was going to teach himself to stand back and take a deep breath so that when things got messed up, he wasn't so overwhelmed by them. His new mantra was going to be, *Don't stress, it's not worth it.*

Chapter 4

Taylor looked over the letter that Ivy had already read. It was indeed from an attorney from her grandparents, and they were both dead. Not that she'd ever had anything to do with them, wouldn't even know them in a room full of people, but they had named her in their will, and there were several insurance policies in her name that she could cash them out. Also, with the will, they said there would be a house and other things that they wanted her to have.

"No explanation on why they were bothering with me after all this time?" Ivy told her that they might well have mentioned it in the will, but they'd have to wait for that. "I wonder if they left my mom anything. I mean, not that she deserves anything right now, but I wondered about it."

"It says there that they didn't mention their daughter Gilda Jane because they had done so much for her before they left her in the care of your father. I believe from what the letter says, they regretted that and the fact that she'd had a child. Not because they thought you'd be wonderful but because, as a child, you'd have to be subject to her oddities." Taylor snorted and asked her if she thought that her mother had oddities or was just a bitch. "For now, I'm going to say oddities. And you have to admit that she is about as odd as it comes."

She'd been hearing from the prison daily. Not to talk to her mom, no, they knew better than that to have her talk to her mother. It was how she was getting along. Or in this case, how she wasn't getting along with the guards or the other prisoners. She was demanding they care for her, and it wasn't going over well.

"I'm to understand that she's not having a good time in prison. She's been put in solitary confinement since she's been there. Just to keep her safe. It's probably a good thing that you said she wasn't to call you anymore, or I'm betting she'd be on the phone to you a great deal." Ivy told her that she was happy to take the calls for her, as that's what she can help with. "So far she's not changed one bit while there, but she's only been there for two weeks already."

"It's been nice not having to have her call me every ten minutes, too. I don't feel the least bit bad about her being sent away, either. She did this to herself. Or her parents did it to her, I can't decide who to blame." She looked over the paperwork again, and Ivy let her. There was a great deal of information in the letter from the attorney, and they'd only touched on a few of the things. "How much money are we talking about here? Not that I need the money, but it might be nice to donate it to some cause that would piss my mother off with."

They both laughed, and she told her how much there was. It was a great deal of money at half a million dollars, but like she said, Taylor was worth billions, and she'd not miss that money if she donated it. She suggested that she divide it up into a couple of charities and be done with it. She said that's what she'd do.

"Also, I want to help out my brother-in-law. Now that Colby has met his mate, I want to help him out. I know that they've just purchased a house to live in, and it's devoid of anything but a bed or two." Ivy was excited about her brother having found his mate, too. Of all of the Tucker men, she loved Colby the best. He was such a good man. "Maybe I can get them a line of credit at the furniture store so that they can get everything they need. Can you make that happen?"

"I can and I will. I know that between the two of them, they have a little money saved; his fishing boat trips are making some great profit for him. But they really need a hand up on their home. Have you seen it yet?" Taylor said that she'd not, but was looking forward to an invite to the house. "Us too. With the new baby coming along now, we've been going out a lot more so that we can be a family again when the new one comes."

"I'm so excited about having Denver's child. We've been practicing a great deal about making one for us." Taylor laughed, and Ivy felt her face heat up. She didn't want to know that about her brother and his wife. But then Taylor had always been outspoken, and it suited her just fine to be with her today. "Anyway, when the time comes, I'm going to be at your doorstep to learn all about having a child with him. It'll be nice that they're all going to be so close, being cousins and all."

"I just hope that Emma and Colby can work things out with each other. They're learning a great deal about each other, which is good. All Hudson and I did was fight right up until we were married. I know that Emma has been having trouble being centered with the two of them so far apart all the time. Perhaps the house that they've gotten together will help out with that."

"There are times when I know just how she feels about being off. She told me that just a touch from Colby and she feels so much better. I hadn't realized that's what happens with us, too. A simple touch and I'm better for the day. I think that's true of humans, too, but I don't know. They seem to fight to the bitter end, humans, I mean." Taylor nodded and said that's what she'd been feeling too at the beginning of their relationship. "I think we all do that. Just a small touch or a kiss, and it's like the world has balanced out for everyone."

They talked a bit more about the paperwork. Since the attorneys were going to come to her about the reading of the will, they only needed to set up a time to do it. And since Gilda Jean wasn't mentioned only to say that she was getting nothing from the estate, there was no reason for her to be bothered by the attorneys when they came to town. It was funny to her that the couple, Gilda Jean's parents, had moved to Ohio, where things had started for the foundation.

On her way home, she decided that they needed to have a meal in tonight. Asking Hudson what he wanted her to pick up, she wasn't surprised that he asked for Chinese. That was her favorite, too, and they could get enough for leftovers for her to take to work tomorrow. She had him order it, and she would pick it up. The man would know what she loved besides him and get all her favorites along with his. She loved Hudson so much.

When she went by to pick up the diapers that were needed at home, she only had to wait another twenty minutes for the food. Hudson was the stay-at-home dad, and she loved working at the foundation. Not that he didn't work there as well sometimes, but so far her working outside the house was giving them both pleasure like they'd never had in their work and home life like never before. They'd always been living paycheck to paycheck before, with having to pay for child care and working too. This was working out so much better for them both, and they rarely fought about the silly stuff, too. Not really fight, but snip, she supposed.

After dinner, almost too full to move, they put the kids to bed and sat in the living room talking about the family. Hudson was going to take the kids over to the grandparents' tomorrow and hang out while helping with the new rose garden that Denver was helping put in. Thanks to Colby learning how much they missed everyone, they were now spending time with them more than they had before. The elderly couple had done so much for the family that they hated to think about the time when they'd want to move on to the next step of their life voyage.

Going up to bed later than usual, the two of them checked on the children and made their way to their own bedroom. It was a wonderful night, and she couldn't believe how much she'd enjoyed her day. Being an attorney had been all she'd wanted as a child, and now that she had the opportunity to be one, she was the best that she could be. Snuggling up to Hudson, she realized that this baby she was carrying was going to have all the things that the others hadn't, simply because they were happy and had money now to burn. All her life, she had wanted children to go along with her good-paying job, and now that she had both, she couldn't believe her luck. Nothing could have prepared her for the love that she had for her little growing family, and she couldn't have been happier than she was at this moment. Kissing Hudson good night, she went to sleep with a smile on her face.

The next morning dawned rainy and dreary. But with her heart full of love and understanding she didn't see the puddles of rainwater nor the dark clouds that were hanging over the house. She could only see the goodness in the day and was whistling when she got to her office. Working for the foundation kept her busy, but it was the lovely perks of getting to see her family throughout the day that made her feel good.

The first thing she did was pull up her email. Having gone through it, she then got her phone messages together and sorted them out. Still having a wonderful day, she answered the correspondence with a smile until she got to the one from Ronin. He wanted her to call him as soon as she got the message.

Fearful that he was going to tell them that this wasn't working out, she called the number that he gave her with a heavy heart. Just thinking that she was going to have to move back home and start over again made her slightly ill. When put on hold from the household staff that he had, she nearly started biting her nails again. Something that she'd not done in almost two years now.

But she was so nervous.

"Hello, Ivy, my dear. Thanks for getting back to me. I have some contracts that I'd like to send you to go over for the foundation here." She let out a long breath, one that she'd not realized that she'd been holding, and then ended up putting her head between her knees. "Honey? Are you all right? Talk to me please, before I have Parker bring me there to see what—"

"I'm fine. I was just nervous that you were going to tell us that we've done something terribly wrong and you were pulling the works from us." He didn't say anything, and she felt the need to explain more. "I've been having such a wonderful morning until I saw the email from you to call you, and my mind just went into overload. I don't know why it did, but there you have it. I'm sorry to have worried you."

"It's fine. Really, it is, but I'm worried that you would think that from an email. Have we made you feel like we're only going to do this for a little while? I mean, this is a forever job for your family. And you're doing such a good—that's why I wanted you to go over some contracts for me. The attorney here isn't as good as you are, and frankly, I'm sort of jealous that you don't work for us here." She told him that she was only as good as he allowed her to be. "Thank you for that. And I'm sorry that I ruined your good day. It wasn't my intention."

"It's fine, really it is. And my good mood will come back to me soon. I've never whistled before today. In fact, I didn't even know that I could." He laughed with her. "I'm sorry. I really don't know why my mind went there.

Probably in the back of my mind, I was waiting for the other shoe to drop or something like that."

"I understand that. When I first got with my wife, it was difficult for me to get my head wrapped around having a seemingly endless supply of money. And with the investments we've made, including your family, it's come back to us tenfold. We've been very fortunate with the way things are going for both our families." She agreed with him and told him so. "Good. I'll be more careful next time I email you. It didn't have much information in it, so I can see where you might well have gotten the wrong message from me. I'll send those contracts over today, and you should have them by lunch. I hope you're going to have a wonderful lunch too."

"I'm having leftovers from dinner last night. Hudson and I pigged out on Chinese food, and I was able to have enough for today." He laughed and told her that they'd had Chinese food last night, too, yet there were no leftovers. "I don't know what I'd do without having a bit for the next day. It's why we order so much. Perhaps you just need to add more to your order."

"Then we'd be eating that too, I'm afraid." After she received the email containing the contracts, they hung up. Ivy liked to print out contracts so that she could mark them with a red pen when she found things that were wrong. After the first page, she knew that this contract needed to be not just not signed by Ronin, but it needed to have spell check used on it as well. The writer of the contract should never have allowed this to be sent out. Once she was on the second contract, from the same company, she called

Ronin back. This was just ridiculous.

She told him what she'd found and told him that she wouldn't do business with a firm at all that didn't bother to check their work. Ivy told him that she had more red marks on the first page than she'd ever seen on anything but a first draft of one. After pointing out a few of them that she'd found, she also told him that there were too many loopholes in the paperwork that she thought they were trying to fool them into signing something like five million dollars away before the work had even been done.

"I could barely get through it with all the mistakes. And you said your own attorney looked this over? I'd fire him, too. Or her. Whatever made them think that this was going to work for your company makes me think that he should go back to school and learn how a sentence is structured. My goodness, it's—why are you laughing?" He told her that he'd never heard her so worked up before. "Well, if I'm going to approve or disprove something, I want it to be for a good reason. This is just shoddy work all the way around for whoever sent this to you, and then your own attorney for not telling you what a piece of crap this was. You can have me do it. I'd love to talk to the person who thought that this was a good thing to send out. But for your own attorney to tell you whatever he did without mentioning the loopholes, not to mention the errors in it, should be fired."

He was still laughing, and she wanted to smack him. She wouldn't, of course, she wasn't that stupid. He was the king of their kind. But just to have him laughing at her made her see red. But she held her tongue and waited for him to finish.

"I'm sorry." Another bout of laughing before he continued. "I've really enjoyed this and must have needed it more than I thought. I will take the attorney to task once I find out why he did such a crappy job, as you put it, and then perhaps fire him. But for now, I'm going to assume that he didn't see it. Which is worse, I suppose. But I do promise to take care of it as soon as I get him in my office."

"I just don't understand why you thought it to be so funny. What if you had signed this without consulting me? There would have been major setbacks to this." He said that he had been told not to sign it. "Then perhaps he's doing a better job than I thought. But still, to have thought of you reading over this paperwork with all the errors on it makes me a little angry."

"I can tell." He didn't laugh this time, but coughed, and she was sure that he was laughing at her still. "Anyway, if you could write up a letter to me telling me about the mistakes, I'll make sure that my man here gets them. And I can't thank you enough for making my day a bit brighter, too. I needed that badly."

For the next hour, she wrote up a summary about the contract being as objective as she could be without losing her temper again. When she sent it off, making sure that there were no errors on the letter, she got busy with her other business. Today started out good, but now she was worried about Ronin and his contracts. She'd ask him to send them all to her before he signed anything, but she had enough work of her own to take care of.

~*~

Emma was on her first stop when she realized that she wasn't going to be home tonight. And she'd been looking forward to sleeping in her own bed, too. As they were unloading the boxes, she reached out to Colby and let him know that she had to work through the night with unloading, and he said he understood that things came up all the time.

She had wanted him to be mad. Upset that she was breaking a date with him, but he was so calm that she — no, she realized that he was distracted. Like he had too much going on to let her bother him too much.

"What's happened?" He asked her what she meant. *"You're very distracted, and I want to know why? Is there someone with you? Are you unable to speak to me at this time?"*

"I got this letter from Taylor with a check in it. It's for the two of us, but I've not opened it yet." She asked him how he knew there was a check in it. *"Because I can see it, there is just enough opening in the envelope to be able to see it. Want me to open it with you now?"*

"Sure. But if she's firing me, I'm going to be pissed off enough to take the check and shove it up her ass. I'm doing the best job that I can, and I won't have her saying anything differently. Understand?" He told her that he doubted that she'd fire her for any reason, and she'd not do it by mail. *"True, but stranger things have happened, you know."*

"I do know. All right. Give me a second to get this open, and I'll read it to you." She felt the moment that something startled him and was worried about it. *"The check is for half a million dollars, to us both. But it says that it's for Colby and Emma Tucker. I don't know why she'd do that when we're not*

married. *Or we could be in the eyes of the law. They file things like this just so it's taken care of and —* " She said his name.

"*Just read the flipping letter and let's decide on whether or not to murder her for giving us so much money.*" He said that was a good idea. "*Yes, well, I do have them on occasion. Read the letter.*"

"*Dearest Emma and Colby, My grandparents died. Don't be upset with finding out. I didn't know them at all, as they were my mother's parents. They were making it up to me by leaving me this money because I had to put up with their daughter. It would have been nicer to me had I gotten some kind of warning about her, but there is nothing I can do about it now. Anyway, I don't need the money. Nor do I want it. It feels like it's dirty. I want you two to use it to fill out your home.*" Emma asked him how much it would cost to fill out a home. "*I don't know, but I'm betting that there will be leftovers from it. Let me finish this as it's not that much longer.*"

He paused like he was reading it ahead of her, and she nearly told him to read it to her, too. However, he explained how he was working too and couldn't wait to get the fishing trip finished so that he could go home.

"*I know it's a great deal of money, and I know you two will use it wisely. I want you to take this dirty money from me and make it clean again by giving new life to your home. I want to do this for you, and Jack thinks that if anyone would use it wisely and for good, it would be you two. Then she signed it, love Taylor and Jack.*"

"*No matter how you look at it, that's still a lot of money to fill out a house with.*" He said that he knew that too and wouldn't be surprised if she came over and looked at the house when they were finished. *"To check up on us? No, she'd not do that. Even if we were to spend the money on anything but the house, she'd be pleased that she didn't have to deal with it. Don't you think?"*

"I do. I also have a feeling that if we were to tell her no, we didn't need the money, she'd find some other way to give it to us. She thinks like that, too." He also told her that he didn't want to piss her off by turning her down. *"That might cause some trouble with her and Jack, and I want to be able to eat in the restaurant again. Not to mention him helping me on the boat when I need it."*

"Yes, to tell her no wouldn't be smart." While she didn't know how much money Taylor and Jack had, she was sure that it was quite a bit more than what she and Colby had for sure. And Taylor grew up with lots of money, too. She just seemed to be really good at it. *"How do we thank her for the money then?"*

"To do what she wants us to do with it and move on. I don't want her upset with me by going all gushy about things either. I think she sent it to us in the form of a letter so that no one else knows. Not that I'd go around telling them, but I have a feeling that she wanted to do this just for the two of us, and I love her for it." Emma said that she had a feeling that Jack really did know about it and would be proud of himself and her for doing it this way. *"Yes, I told you that we can't lie to one another. She'd tell him so that we could thank him too without causing any trouble."*

They talked a bit more about the check and what they were going to do with it, and decided that she was in a better frame of mind than when she spoke to him at first.

Sometimes in the middle of the night, she would reach out to him just to hear his mind at work. It was no less than he'd done to her when he'd been in her mind, but for some reason, she didn't feel the need to get snippy with him about it. Instead, she told him what she had been doing, and he laughed.

"You should talk to me. I mean, I'm more than likely awake pining for you anyway." She asked him if he really was. *"Yes. All I can think about is loving you and making you mine. I'm not going to rush you into anything, but I did want you to know what I'm feeling. I miss you too."*

"It's funny you should say that because I miss you as well. Very much so." He asked her if she was all right with that. *"I am. And I'll tell you something else. I'm falling in love with you, too. Every time I talk to you, it's all I can do not to blurt out my feelings for you. And I have a lot of them."*

"I don't want to make you mad at me or anything, but all I can think about is making love to you. Tasting your body and feeling yours next to mine." She said that she'd been having the same thoughts herself. *"Good. Maybe while we're both home this time, we can talk a little more about that part of our relationship. I know that I'd like to have your thoughts on it."*

"My thoughts are that we should buy us a big bed for the house and break it in. I've no problem whatsoever in telling your sister-in-law how much that money helped us to be a better couple, do you?" He laughed, and she felt it all the way to her toes. It wasn't a humor-filled laughter but one filled with promise and need. *"I want you, Colby. Like I've never wanted a man before."*

"My lust-filled brain has made my cock hard. And the

thought of what you look like naked has my cock dripping too. I'm going to have to take another cold shower or jack off again with your words in my head." Christ, she thought, this was a dangerous topic while she was driving. She told him that. "*I never thought of that. I'm sorry, babe. I'll behave myself. If you will. For now.*"

For the rest of her trip to the next store, she told him what kind of furniture she wanted in their new house. The first thing they were going to need was a bed, but they skipped over that for now. A kitchen table with chairs was something that she noticed they needed as well, since they'd been standing at the counter while eating pizza the other night. Their first meal in their new home together had been the best pizza that she'd ever eaten. And she loved it.

By the time she was being unloaded at the next store, she was exhausted. The sexual talk got her worked up, and now here she was driving a big rig while trying to get her body to quiet down and behave itself. She would know better next time in talking like that over the link they had, and it would be best if she were to have a hint as to what his body looked like.

The next store was nearly closing time when she got there. Almost as soon as she was getting ready to leave to find a place to park, she saw them locking up their doors. One more drop off in the morning and she could get back to home base and be off for the next three days. Having enough crew around to take some of the loads was certainly making her life better and easier, too.

After parking, she made herself something to eat.

Since she had a full-sized refrigerator, she had a nice-sized freezer compartment as well. Pulling out one of the meals that her mom had made her had her homesick again. The pasta and sauce hit the spot for her in more ways than just filling her belly. It made her think about how much she missed her mom, too.

Getting ready for bed, she left out some treats for Crumble. He didn't make an appearance right away, but she wasn't worried about him. He had enough magic that he could pop in and out of the rig whenever he wanted. And she was sure that he had a family that he missed as well. Just as she was settling into her big bed, she thought of Colby. He answered her just as if she'd called out for him.

"I love you very much, Emma Tucker. We are married in the name of the law. Someone had it filed away so that we didn't have to mess with it if we didn't want to. But that doesn't mean that we can't do the deed later down the line." She thanked him for that and told him good night. *"Good night, love. I'll see you tomorrow for a fun-filled day of shopping for things for the new house."*

"We need to make a list." He agreed and said that he'd started it off with the number of bedrooms. *"Good idea. And whatever things we'll need in the kitchen as well. Tea maker for sure, and I noticed that you don't drink coffee either, but we should have one just in case my mom comes by. She doesn't drink it often, but enough that she needs it once in a while."*

While talking to Colby again, she started to drift off. She really was tired and just wanted to get home to be with him. So when she yawned for the fifth time in as many minutes, he told her again that he loved her and closed the connection. One more drop off and she'd be going home. It had never sounded so good before meeting Colby.

Chapter 5

He had thirty-three applicants for the jobs on the boats. Denver had put a post up at the foundation, and there were people who wanted to try out the job. The first thing that he had to do was interview them, as his brother had already done a background check on all of them and had started the process of drug testing as well. That certainly made his job a good deal easier. Then he was going to have to train them on how to work aboard a boat for several days at a time while their guests fished. His last night on the boat had proven they needed to be up for anything.

They were fishing off the starboard side of the boat when a large wave knocked them around in the water. Looking to see what it was, they were amazed to see two whales cresting the water and making waves. Then they saw the baby one and stood in awe as they all three swam around them while the men watched. It was the best sighting that he'd ever seen in all the years he'd been hired out as a fishing boat captain.

But for now, he was going to get cleaned up and go pick up Emma so that they could go to the house and make notes. He didn't do anything without notes, and today wasn't going to be the exception. It took them three hours to go over the house and make a list of the things they were going to need. Christ, he was exhausted just thinking about what had to be purchased.

Depositing the check had caused a bit of a stir at the bank. While there, they decided to open an account together and make sure that they had the cards that would make it easier to spend the money. They had to get approval from Taylor to make sure that she had signed over a check that large, but all in all, they got it squared away in a reasonable time.

The first thing they did was go to the furniture store. They were then going to go to the appliance center to get the other things on their list. They'd not realized that the washer and dryer had come with their house, but after having it inspected, they were told that it was an older model and wouldn't last that much longer. That was going to be something they'd need right away, and they were going to get one for both the first floor and the second floor, as the house was designed that way.

By six-thirty, they were starving and had barely made a dent in their shopping spree. They knew that they needed five-bedroom suites, but decided after looking at the prices of them that they'd just get what was necessary for now. That meant a bed for the master and one other bed for one of the bedrooms on the floor. That way, someone could spend the night if they wished, and they'd not have to sleep on the floor. The living room furniture was perfect for the room they were going to use it in.

They ended up with two couches rather than one couch and a love seat. The room was large enough to hold the two of them, but it was the large screened television that they purchased for the fall sports season that they were the most happy with. He didn't actually think that they'd watch more than just sports on it, as neither of them seemed to enjoy watching anything else.

The kitchen was put off until they got to the appliance store. They did have a dishwasher, but they didn't know how old it was or anything about it other than it had been put in the last year. The house had had a large family in it before they bought it, and they were worried that it might well have been used a great deal. Buying another one with all the other things seemed like a smart idea.

"We're having this all delivered, right? I mean, I could go around and pick things up, but it would take longer as I would have to get a trailer to take with me and figure out parking." Colby agreed that having it all delivered would be faster and smarter in the event something happened to it while in transit. "You don't think that I'd mess up our stuff, do you? I'm totally offended." They both laughed.

"We're paying extra to have them bring it into the house. I don't want to ask my family for help as they've been so busy lately with everything else going on with their jobs." Emma agreed with him on that. "Good. This way, we don't have to complain about our backs being too delicate when it comes time to move things."

There were other things that they purchased when they realized that they needed them. A vacuum was one of the things they hadn't thought about. Then there were lamps around the rooms. The bedrooms would need some, too, but like the bedroom suites, they were going to wait until they found some that they really liked and not settle for something just because they wanted to get it all done.

By nine, they were about halfway through their lists but too exhausted to go on. They had gotten linens for the master and the extra bed, towels, and extras for the bathrooms. They'd nearly forgotten shower curtains, and if not for the woman in front of them saying she needed them, they would not have been able to take a shower until they had some. Then there were things like silverware and dishes.

They found a set of dishes that they liked that would be for every day. They were plain white without a design on them. But for the dining room, they weren't agreeing on what kind to get. In the end, that was another thing that they put off until they could agree and handled the silverware by tossing a coin. Emma won the toss and picked out the set that would be in their forever home.

"I'm guessing that with you being a lion, we won't have to worry about pests?" Colby laughed and said that even little house cats wouldn't be around all that much unless they were brought up on the land. "I figured as much. Cats are pretty territorial, so I can see that they'd not like to have to fight for a window seat in our house. What else can we expect with you being a lion? Anything that I should know?"

"Like little cats, we like to play in the yard. I won't shift in the house unless it's necessary because I would damage the floor. But we might chase a butterfly and never harm it. Or just play in the water. Our cats seem to really enjoy being in the water at times." She told him that she couldn't wait to see his cat. "When we get to the house, I'll shift for you. You should really get to know all the cats in the family, so that way you can tell us apart. Not that it's important that you do. If we're all together and as our cats, that usually means that something is going on that's important that we are our other selves."

"I can't imagine what it would be like to shift into something else. I've thought about it, and I want to see you do it. You're going to be larger than you are as a man, correct? That's what I heard from my friend who is a wolf shifter." He told her that Denver is larger than he was, and then Ronin, as the king, is even larger. "I forgot about him being king. It must be really special to have a friendship with the king of your kind."

"The next time they're in town, I'll make sure you get to meet them. You'll love them as much as we do. They've done so much for us now that I don't know how we would ever repay them. Thanks mostly to Denver getting things all gathered up and talking to them. We only came out here to help them, and they made everything else happen for us to be a family." She just snorted. "What? Don't you believe me?"

"I think that you guys were a family—a tight family before all this came to be. You are so close to one another that it sort of makes me jealous of how much you guys depend on one another and really seem to love each other. I've never seen a group of people hug as much as you guys do when you're together." He said that they love one another. "You respect one another, too. And that is what makes your family special above all others."

"Thank you for that." They were driving back to her mom's home when he decided that they needed to go by the house for one thing. "We didn't get the measurements for the washer and dryers, and I want to make sure they're going to fit. I won't be a minute."

He was just going to run in and measure and come back out, but she decided that since they were there, they might as well put the things that they weren't going to have delivered in the house. There were all kinds of boxes that they had, mostly it was kitchen things like the tea maker and the coffee pot, but by the time they got it all in the house, they were both hungry again.

"Will we have staff, you think?" She was putting together some sandwiches for them that had been put in the fridge just this morning. "I'm glad that mom suggested that we have food for when we're going in and out of here."

They both ate two of them, and Colby was on his third when he realized that he'd not answered her about the staff. He told her that they'd need at least a cook and someone to dust and clean up after them because they both worked full-time and were out of the house sometimes for days.

"I would hate to have to come home to a dusty house with all our things lying about. Wouldn't you?" She told him that she didn't want to have to cook every night either. It was hard enough when she was on the road to cook herself a meal. "If not for the clients eating on the boat, I don't know what I'd do about cooking. The galley is small compared to the kitchen we have now." He put things away since she'd been the one who put the food together. "I don't care for chips; however, I do like a good veggie tray once in a while. What about you?"

"I love chips, but not too often. I don't buy a big bag because once I have my fill of them, I don't want any more for months. They usually go stale before I ever get back around to them. Having a cook is all right with me." He agreed with her and helped her break down the boxes that the appliances came in. "Another thing that I don't care for is a salad with fruit in it. You know, like those salads that you get with chicken and strawberries in it? I don't want fruit in my lettuce."

"I have to agree with you on that one. I don't want meat in my salad either. Just salad things." They were laughing with each other, talking about their likes and dislikes. There wasn't a lot of food that he wouldn't eat, but there were things that he'd eat if necessary, but he didn't have to enjoy it. "I love chili, but I don't understand the people who drink chocolate milk with it. I want soda with my chili."

"I love chili in the fall. White chili is my favorite." She explained to him what that was, and he thought that he could enjoy that too. White chili sounded really good. "With cornbread, too. Or those cheesy crackers. I love them smashed up in my bowl."

When things were put on the counter like they wanted them to be, they decided that the washer and dryer would indeed fit in the slots made for them, and they took the boxes out to the garage. That's where they'd been putting things that they brought by the house that needed to be put away. He couldn't wait until things started to arrive and be put away. He wanted to stay at the house in the worst sort of way.

With everything being delivered over the next couple of days, they figured that they could be living in the house full-time in a few days. The only thing that they might not have was staff, and they were both willing to forgo that so long as they were home. He was going to get with Denver and see if he could put an ad in the paper for one for them.

"We'll need a cook as we said, but staff? I don't know what to do about them. I wouldn't even know what to call whoever comes in and dusts the house for us." She said she thought they were called domestics. "That's not a nice word to call someone, is that?"

"I don't know where I heard that from, but I'd take my cues from Taylor and Jack. They have a full staff all the time, including a butler. I'm sure we don't need one of those, do we?" He said that he didn't have any idea, but thought it was a good idea to ask Taylor, as she'd had staff her entire life. "Good, I'll talk to her tomorrow." She leaned against the wall where they were standing, looking at the washer and dryer area. "I'm exhausted, Colby. How about we go to our homes and start again tomorrow? Once things are put into place, we'll have a better idea of what else we're going to need for the house."

"I agree. And as much as I'd like to spend the night with you here, there is only a small mattress up on the second-floor bedroom, and that's not even big enough for me." She leaned against him and yawned. "All right. Let's get you home before you fall asleep standing up. Neither of us wants that."

He was tired himself and couldn't wait to go back to the condo and get some sleep. He'd not been sleeping well on the boat, and he thought it had a lot to do with the fact that he was in flux right now. They didn't have a house, nor did he particularly care for the condo anymore. He just wanted things settled.

After dropping off Emma, it was all he could do to let her go into the house alone; he went to the condo. He didn't even call it home anymore as he realized that a house was a home for him. Getting a shower was first on his list, and after that, he fell into his bed. He'd not set an alarm but was too exhausted to get up and take care of it now. Colby was usually an early riser and hoped that he would be tomorrow, too.

~*~

Taking a shower, Emma tried to get her sore muscles to cooperate with her in getting ready for the day. She'd helped unload a little bit of her truck yesterday morning, and she was feeling it. If just moving a few boxes had her that sore, she was going to have to hit the gym a little bit so that she wouldn't be feeling like this again. Her shoulders were very sore.

Colby had called her and woke her up, telling her that he was running behind. Well, so was she. Usually an early riser, too, she couldn't believe that she'd slept until nine-thirty when she was normally up by six. Getting out of the shower, she heard someone in the kitchen with her mom and decided that it had to be Colby, and rushed through dressing herself with magic so that she could go out and see him. It wasn't Colby, but Jack, and he was there to talk to her.

"Sometimes I have a few leftovers at the restaurant, and I wondered if you might like to take them with you on runs? I can have it wrapped up and ready for you to go if you want them. Otherwise, they just go to waste." She told him that it would be fantastic. "Great. I even got you a couple of lunch taker things that I can fill up for you. You can put them in the freezer, too."

"That's great. Mom usually makes me something with her leftovers, too, and to be frank, I'm sick of sandwiches. I can eat them, but a real meal is what I crave. It reminds me of home." Jack said that he had a couple in the car right now and would get them for her. On his way out, she asked him if she could talk to him, too, about staffing. "We know that we're going to need them as we both work full time, but we're not sure how much we might need. Not to mention, what we would call them when they do work for us."

After putting the food in the freezer—they were fried chicken and mashed potatoes in one, and the other had meatloaf with the same side dish that she could have with a roll or a couple of slices of bread as a sandwich. She was about as excited for those as she was for anything she'd eaten on the road before.

"We have a cook and butler. There are other staff members around, but I couldn't tell you what they're called. A gardener, which I recommend because you guys have a yard the size of ours, and if you're working, you're not going to get to it. Also, we have all the land around the house that you guys won't have to mess with. There are gardens that are worked year-round that keep the house self-sufficient." She said they weren't at that point yet. "It's a long process that needs to be put in place if you plan on not ever going to the grocery store. But I love it. I've been using some of the excess in the restaurant, and it's been great."

She asked him if she thought that Taylor might be able to help. He looked relieved. Like, having to help her was too much for him to do. She laughed at him when he thanked her several times for not making him name everyone who worked for them. He was only just getting around to getting their names straight.

"I do know that someone comes in and does the beds for us. I hate making a bed, so it's nice to have it done up daily. There is someone, too, who cleans the bathrooms. They could be the same person, but as I said, I'm only just getting used to having people around me all the time. Taylor is used to it, as that's what she grew up with, but not me. I just know that I couldn't do it without their help behind the scenes, so to speak. And I make sure that I thank them every time I see them." Colby showed up just as she was sitting down to the breakfast that her mom had made for her. Colby joined her as he'd missed getting anything to eat, as he'd been without milk for two days now. "That's another thing that I love. I don't have to ever worry about there being nothing to eat around the house. I don't know if they do it because of me, but whenever I go to the fridge to get something to snack on, there are sandwiches that I can take without bothering the staff."

They talked about the staffing issue that they might run into, but Jack said to them numerous times that Taylor would know what to do. But it was funny to see how embarrassed he got when he talked about never seeing them walking around when something was suddenly taken care of.

"I don't know that we'll need all the staff that you have, but we're going to start out right on this. Knowing what we will need will be half the battle, I think." Jack said that he was learning the gardening aspects of the house so that he could incorporate things into the restaurant, too. "I know that's something that you've always wanted. To have fresh for your patrons."

When they were ready to go, she asked Jack if he wanted to go to the new house to have a look around. He declined, saying that he had to go to the fish market today as it was Friday. He always tried to have fish on Fridays so that people would enjoy it. After a good hug goodbye, they set off to go to the house to wait on things to start coming in. Also, they were going to do some online shopping for the few things that they'd forgotten to get, like measuring cups and kitchen knives. Emma called Taylor on her way to the house to see if she could be more helpful. Asking her if she was busy was the first thing out of her mouth.

"Never too busy for you guys. How's the house shopping going? I don't envy you doing that. I'm glad that when I moved in with Grandma, she had everything that we needed to have a nice home to live in. Though it is a big house, we seemed to have a lot of things that are just around when we need them." Emma told her that they thought they were doing all right and thanked her again for the money. "No need for that. Like I said, I didn't need it right now, and perhaps one day you might find yourself in a situation where you can pay it forward to someone else. That would make me happy."

She got the help with the domestics, what people working in the house were called when they did the jobs around. Taylor said that they'd need a butler only because he can answer the door when you're out and take messages for them.

"With the two of you working so much, much more than I am, you'll need someone to be able to run the house. He'll run the house for you, while whoever you have in the kitchen will run that part of the house for you. It's a seamless operation with the two of them working together." Taylor also said that it's nice to have someone around who can make up beds and clean the other parts of the house that they'll use daily. "It's nice coming home from work, and things are just so. I don't know that I could be gone for several days at a time without having someone around to take care of the small stuff for me. It's very organized as well."

"We'll talk about that, too." Taylor asked them what they were doing for dinner tonight and invited them over for a meal. "I don't know. We've been just grabbing whatever is in the refrigerator when we get hungry. A good home-cooked meal sounds good." Colby agreed.

"Good. We'll have something comforting tonight, and I'll tell the cook. It'll be nice having someone to pamper tonight. We've been sort of taking the evenings easy for the last week, what with my Grandma gone. She still has about two weeks left on her cruise." Emma said she'd love to go on one of those, too, someday. "We should do it as a family. The cruise liner won't know what hit them when we all converge on the buffet one night."

They were still laughing when they pulled up in front of the house. There was already a truck there waiting for them with the washer and dryer sets. She couldn't wait to get a load of towels in so that they could take a shower at the end of the day today. They were going to be sweaty if they didn't when they went to Jack's house tonight.

The furniture came earlier, and they were excited about that. As things were being put in the rooms they'd purchased it for, things were starting to look better. Having the couches in the living room made the entire room feel warmer, and she couldn't wait to see the television set up so the room would be considered complete.

They knew that they'd find things that they didn't buy for the house, and it was Colby who went out to get them some laundry detergent for the towels and sheets. She figured that she could have the beds made up after they arrived, and that would give them a place to sleep tonight. However, if she had anything to say about sleeping in the bed, there would be little of that going on. She wanted to make love to Colby so badly.

By the time lunch time rolled around, they were on their second load of laundry, and the beds were being put together. She was glad that they'd gotten an extra dresser for their room, as it filled the space out nicely. She made a list of things that they were going to need for the bathroom—new toothbrushes and paste, little things like that, and sent the order off to be delivered tomorrow. If she was honest with herself, she loved the fact that they were starting out with all new stuff for their first home together and was excited to break things in, too. At three in the afternoon, a woman by the name of Carol Anne showed up and said she was the cook. Taylor had sent her over to get their kitchen set up and to work for them. It was the best news they had had all day, other than the furniture being delivered one day early because they had time.

After telling Carol Anne their work schedule and what they liked to eat, she said she'd have breakfast for them in the morning if the delivery of food could make it out to the house. She also said that she'd take over ordering the things that she'd need—pots and pans, knives, and whatnot so that it would be things she was used to using. Emma was fine by that. One less thing that she had to worry about at the end of the day. Telling her that they were having dinner out tonight had her laughing. First night dinner would be tomorrow night, she told her, so long as they didn't mind comfort food. They were both all right with that.

It was nearly six o'clock when the household was finished for today. They were both armed with lists that they needed, and she found that ticking off the kitchen stuff made her life easier all the way around. As soon as tomorrow, most of the things that she'd been ordering all day would be delivered, and she couldn't have been happier.

"I have to go out on Thursday. But I'll be back on Friday afternoon. It's just a couple of men who want to get used to the idea of going fishing with someone else at the helm." Emma told Colby that she'd be back on Friday late, as she had to go out Friday morning to deliver to a couple of stores. "Then we'll have things working by the weekend. Do you have any routes this weekend?"

"No. I'm off, thanks to Taylor, so we can get the things set up that we have purchased. I'm going to move my clothing over sometime over the weekend, too. Are you going to move in to be here full-time?"

"Yes, but to be honest, I don't have all that much. Mostly shorts for the trips out and t-shirts that have the company name on them. Tucker Fishing seemed like a good name for me, and I'm finding it to be easy to remember, too. I'm hoping everyone who needs a good holiday remembers it as well." She said that it suited him. "Thanks. I like it too."

"I have a lot of shorts too. Driving a truck doesn't mean that I get to see all that many people who care about what I'm wearing." He laughed and said he could see that happening. "But I do have a couple of dresses that I've always had. Just in the event of something happening, and I need a little black number to wear. I have to dress up for you one of these days."

"I'd love that." She got a hug from him that she'd not realized that she needed. "We'd better get started or we'll be here all night again. Just a few boxes to cut down, and then we'll have to have trash service hooked up as well. Maybe I'll see if Taylor wants it for her cardboard box project of recycling them. That would be great if we don't have them in the landfill."

They talked about things that they still needed, and she told him how she would just think of something and order it. So there would be a lot of boxes coming in yet. The two of them were having such a good time that she almost didn't want it to end. But duty called, and they were expected at Taylor and Jack's house, and she was also looking forward to it, too.

Chapter 6

Dinner was fantastic as he knew it would be, and sitting out on their deck watching the trees sway was just what he needed in order to relax. Colby felt himself drifting off when his brother sat down next to him and poked him in the ribs. He asked him what that was for.

"You're snoring. Are we so boring that you have to fall asleep now?" They both laughed, and Colby sat up higher on his seat. He'd have to get these kinds of seats for their back deck, too. They were so comfortable. "I wanted to ask you something about your boats. When are you going to get numbers two and three?"

"I can only do them one at a time because I have to train people. As much as I'd love to have them both at the same time, it's not feasible with me having to do all the training." He asked about his crew now. "I'm losing one of them to pregnancy in about a week. She's been helping train her replacement, and it's been good to have that. And Douglas has been doing a good job on his own, so I'm going to have him take out one of the trips in the next couple of days. I'll just be crew and not for me to take over."

"That's wonderful. So you can put him in charge of the next boat." He asked him why he was talking about him getting the extra boats. "I'm going to open a catering job with our sister, Dakota. She is doing really well, and we thought that you could be our test dummy."

"Gee, thanks." Jack laughed at him. "What do you need me to do? You know that I'll be glad to help you in any way that I can."

"Nothing that you're not doing already. I love that we can help each other with different types of meals." He said he'd been meaning to talk to him about it. "I'm betting it has to do with the full menu and dinner options."

"It does. It's too much work for us when it's over. Usually, the clients will go to their room or hang out, but sometimes they want to get in a bit more fishing. With the crew being so limited, it's difficult to clean up after a big meal and take care of their needs as well. I think I'd like to take that off the menu." Jack said he'd been thinking the same thing, only that it's not being used as much to make it worth their while. "Great. Then we agree on it. What else do you have to tell me? I have a feeling that it's more with the boat than the food that you've been providing for us."

"I want to rent you for a day." He said that he could do that for him. "I want you to charge me, too. I'll give you a good review, but I want to go out and see the ocean from where you are daily. I don't care if I fish or not, but a day on the ocean with Taylor."

"I can do that too. And since that's all you want to do, I can book you guys in for next week. I have a spot open that I was saving for the day off, but this will be so much better. Maybe I'll be able to bring Emma, and we can make a whole day of it." His brother loved the idea.

"I'll have gear in the event you want to try your hand at fishing. But it's not a big deal if you only want to see the sights. They're too wonderful to put into words. And I'm not charging you, idiot. You've helped us way more than a trip will cost us."

"I don't want you to think that's the reason we did this. It really has made Taylor feel better about the money that came to her. And next Monday, an attorney is coming to town to read the will from her grandparents that she's named in." Colby asked if she was going to be all right with that. "I think so. She doesn't know them and sort of dislikes them for what they did about her mother and dad. But she's willing to forgive them if they tell her that they're sorry for how they unloaded Gilda Jane off on her dad without telling him about her oddities."

"Oddities? Is that what you're calling it?" Again, they both laughed, and he felt better about the whole thing with her grandparents and their deaths. "Have you heard anything about how Gilda Jane is doing in prison? I'm betting she's not having a good time about it. I know that if I were her my cellmate, I might have to knock her around a bit."

"She's been in solitary confinement most of the time she's been there. She causes situations where they have to get her off the floor for one reason or another. There isn't any way that she's supposed to be allowed to call here, but she does bitch about what Taylor isn't doing for her when she should be." Colby said that the one time he'd had anything to do with her, he couldn't believe how selfish she'd been. "Tell me about it. The one time I had to deal with her on my own, she had slapped a little boy for telling her she wasn't invited to his birthday party. It was at the complex where she lived. She just sat there with them like she'd been invited and was getting in their way. Stupid woman. I'm glad that she's gone out of our lives. The whole thing about her telling us that she was going to live with us to keep us from having children still scares me a bit."

"I don't blame you. You heard about my caller and his wanting to use my boat to rid himself of a couple of bodies. Every time my phone rings, I still get a little tensed up about it." Jack told him that he'd never be able to do what he does without a great deal of fear. "I'm all right now. I have Cup with me, and she makes sure that all my trips are good ones."

"That's good to know." Handing him a bottle of water when he asked for it had them leaning back on the chairs. His brother asked him if he'd gotten what he needed from Taylor about staffing. "I've noticed around here, since I talked to you both, how many people actually work for our house. There must be twenty or so people doing things around here to make me think that this house is perfectly ran. I hope she suggested a butler. They are the ones who make sure that the house is in good working order. And if I need an answer to something, even something that's not house-related, he can steer me in the right direction."

"I've noticed them around here, too. They do their job quietly and without any kind of trouble or drama. It's like they might have a link to each other to get things finished up." Jack told him that's what he thought too, but there aren't that many shifters that work for the house. "Our new cook is a tiger. She reminds me of Grandma behind the sink in the kitchen. I won't mess with her at all. She scares me a bit."

He'd forgotten what it was like to have family around all the time. He missed just being able to sit and talk to his family when there was nothing going on. They were all taking turns going out to the grandparents' house, and his turn was coming up soon. He'd heard that the rose garden was put in and looked beautiful around the house, and that Grandma could be seen out there picking blooms several times a week. There were plans in the works about getting all together with them and making a day of it. Jack was going to be providing the food, and they'd grill out all day to feed everyone. He was looking forward to it as well. Just like tonight, just to hang out with someone from the family.

At ten, they were headed back to the house. The beds were all made up, and he was looking forward to sleeping in his own room with Emma. He didn't know if they'd have sex or not; she'd been complaining about her sore muscles all evening and couldn't believe how just moving around a few boxes had done her in. He pointed out that she'd been moving things around at the house, too, and that could be a large part of it.

"I guess so. But it's my shoulders that hurt the most." He took her hand into his much larger one and kissed the back of it. "That's very nice of you. I could really get used to having you around all the time. You make me feel special."

"You are special to me." She kissed his hand, and they parted at the car to get in. "How about we don't do anything at the house tonight but gather up our clothing so we can stay there all the time now? I have to go out in the morning to do paperwork, and I know that you have stuff to do in the courthouse tomorrow. I didn't know that you had to renew your license at the courthouse around here."

"I don't have to, but it's one of the perks of living in a smaller town. I can get it all done in one place. I have to register my rig too tomorrow, so it's like killing two birds with one stone." He said he understood getting things done. "I'm to understand that you might be getting a second boat soon. Will that take you away from home more?"

"No, I'll run it like a second location, very few for the start. My business has really taken off, and I'm thinking that I need the second boat now rather than later." She said she was proud of him. "Thank you. I never thought this was going to happen, and I can't believe that it's happening now that I need to expand. It's a thrill to know that I'm going to be a bigger business soon."

He hated to drop her off at her mom's home. He'd been wanting to sleep with her for weeks now. But he knew he was right in doing things this way. If they made love tonight, neither of them would be getting up early enough to get to their appointments, nor would they be fit to work the day after, with being sore. He knew for a fact that they'd be sore, too. It was something that his brothers had complained about after spending the night with their mates. He wasn't going to allow himself to be not just sore while working, but too tired to function throughout the day, too. He thought he was a good deal smarter than his brothers in that respect. At least he hoped so.

"It should only take me about an hour to pack my clothing up. Then a couple of more to get the rest of the things out of the condo. There isn't that much there I'm going to be bringing over to our home, but — don't you just love the sound of that? Our home. Anyway, I will need to have it cleaned up so it can be rented again. Did I tell you that Taylor owns all the condos in that area?" Emma told him that she'd known that but had forgotten. "What will your mom say about you moving out so soon? I'm betting that she'll be lonely again."

"I think that she'll be happy for us. She's enjoying her time alone in the house now that she has a job that she can go to. Also, she wants to get herself a dog, someone that she can talk to while I'm gone." He asked if it was going to be a puppy so that it could get used to him while it's still little. "Oh. I never thought of that. I'll tell her about you being a big bad cat and him being a little doggie. That way, it can be like you said, it'll get used to you being around."

When he dropped her off, he went to the condo to pack up his things. There really wasn't all that much, and he didn't even fill a box with his clothing. Putting his toothbrush in another box with his toiletries, he was finished but for the three pieces of furniture that were still there. He was going to donate it all to some charity and be done with it. Since they had the money, they were starting over with all new things at their house.

Getting into bed, he had to calm himself down several times before he could get his body to relax enough to welcome sleep. He was mentally revved up but physically exhausted. He was kind of looking forward to being on the boat so he could rest a bit. Tomorrow, he was just a crew hand while his buddy ran the trip. He was both excited and disappointed in that going on. He wanted it all to himself but knew that if he wanted to expand fully, he couldn't run two or three boats without help. He did wonder just as he was drifting off if he'd be able to have more than just the three that he was counting on to run the sea for fishmen.

Tomorrow would tell if he could leave someone in charge of the other boat while he was working too. It would be great to know if he could do it and sit back too, without trying to take over. That part made him very nervous about the trips, but he had all the confidence in the world in his partner. Well, not all the confidence, but most of it. He was very nervous about letting the reins go.

~*~

It took Emma most of the morning to get her things done. She'd been standing in line for nearly thirty minutes when she was told that she couldn't get her rig registered here, that she had to go to the bursar's office to get it done. Standing in line for another twenty minutes had her in a crappy mood, but she kept telling herself that she was getting things done that needed to be done, and she didn't have anything more to worry about after this. Not until next year at least.

Stretching her neck muscles, she was glad that her shoulders were better today. She'd been told that her grandma wouldn't have the aches and pains of someone her age, and Emma thought that she was getting them all. But she did feel better today, and that was something she'd been hoping for.

Not that she'd admit to anyone that she was happy that they'd not spent the night together last night, but she was happier about it than she thought she might be. With her having to get up early this morning, she was able to get going quickly without having to want to stay in bed with Colby. When the two of them came together, she was going to make sure that she had all night and into the next day with him. She was so in love with the man that it boggled her mind that it had even happened.

She didn't want him to be around at first. But his kindness and calmness won her over. He'd never pushed her into anything, but was a calming force for her, and she loved him for that. She'd had a feeling that he was only out for one thing, and that was sex with her, but he'd proven himself to be a gentleman by waiting until she was ready for him. And boy oh boy was she ready for him to take her. But things about their busy life kept getting in the way.

Tonight, she had plans for his body. She was going to strip him down and make sure he knew what it was like to have a naked woman in his bed. Laughing, she wondered what he would think when she was naked in his bed. She didn't think she was all that much to look at.

Her breasts were too small, and her hips flared kind of widely from the waist down. She knew that she had strong legs; it helped that she was forever loading and unloading her trailer every day and hooking up and unhooking at the docks. She kept herself in pretty good shape, but it was her body that disappointed her as a whole.

She hoped that he was so needy that he'd not notice. But of course he would, simply because it would be hard to hide a body when it was downed in nothing but a layer of skin. Laughing to herself, she thought about what she'd seen in the mirror when she'd taken a shower this morning. There were all kinds of small and large bruises on her body from moving things around at the new house that she'd not realized that she had. Especially the one that was on her shoulder. She must have banged it good on something to make the dollar-sized bruise there on the top of her arm.

Deciding that she needed to start running again, she thought about doing it on the beach. Her mom had a nice beachfront property that was long and wide. Wondering if she could convince Colby to run with her, she thought that he was in good enough shape as it was from working on the trips that he was on. She didn't know how it worked, but she had to figure that he was getting a lot of exercise on the boat, which kept him in good shape.

By the time she was on her only run today, she was ready for a nap. She'd slept well last night and the night before, so she didn't understand why she was so exhausted. Then there was the fact that she'd been getting up earlier, too. Stretching her muscles to make sure she didn't get any sorer, she drove to the shop to get unloaded so that she could go back home and finish up packing. Since most of her things were in the rig, as she'd been living full-time in it for the last five years, she didn't have much in the way of clothing or other things at her mom's house that she thought that she'd need at the new house.

Excitement always made her smile at the thought of moving into the bigger home. She'd never thought that she'd want to live in a five-bedroom home as she'd had so little space in the rig. But the fact that she was looking forward to having so much room made her think that she could get used to it quickly. Plus, there was room at the new house where she could park her rig, and it wouldn't be an eyesore out in the open like it was at her mom's home. There were a lot of perks like that she was looking forward to.

Another thing was the pool. She'd never had a pool before and was looking forward to having a nice swim after a long day in the truck. The ocean was fairly close to them, but the thought of all that sand and people made her think that she'd be using their pool more than the beach. She also liked the fact that there was room on the property for a garden.

She'd never been one to garden at all. Not even to have a flower bed. But there was something so appealing about having fresh things to bring in from a little garden that was making her excited to have it. She knew that she'd not have a lot of time to devote to something larger than a few things, but she was definitely going to grow some things so that she could go out and pick something when she wanted it. The house already had a few fruit trees on the property, so there was that. But she wanted some carrots to grow as well as a few tomatoes.

On her way back after getting her back load, she was making good time and thought that she'd be finished up before one. That made it so that she could take her things to the house and get them put away before Colby got there, and she thought that they'd have dinner at the house on their first night staying there.

Gathering up some of the things from the rig, she made her final trip into the house just as Colby contacted her. He said things were going very well without him being in charge. He also told her that he'd be staying tonight at the house too, as the charity company was coming by to pick up the last of his things this afternoon. That his brother was going to be there to let them in and lock up.

"That's wonderful. I have my things there now. I was hoping you'd be home for dinner." He said that it might be as late as eight o'clock for her not to wait on him. *"I won't if you think you're going to be that late. But please be careful coming home."* He promised her that he would be.

"I have to go by and pick up some things that I didn't have at home that I've been putting off buying. It's just a few things like deodorant and toothpaste. I should have gotten it sooner, but I hate shopping for things like that. It's nearly impossible to just get it and get out of the store without getting a hundred things that I don't know if I need or not." She laughed at him, telling him that she never went anywhere without her list. *"I have trouble remembering that I need shoe laces, too. It's one of those*

things that you never remember until you're putting on your shoes. But I have a list now and I'm going to stick to it."

"I'll meet you at the house when you're finished. Mom is excited to have the house to herself, I think. She was telling me that she's going to go out and get herself something to work on at home. She wants to try needlepoint." He said that would be wonderful for her. *"I hope she likes it. Mom seems to think that if she doesn't have anything to do, she'll grow old before her time. I don't know about that, she's seemed to be young for her age since I've known her."*

"I forgot that you were her stepdaughter." She said that her dad had met her mom when she'd been very young, and it had been the two of them since he passed away. *"I remember you telling me that. It's a good relationship that the two of you have that people don't even notice that you're not related."*

They talked a bit more, and he said that he had to go and get the galley cleaned up now that dinner was over for the people. There was a woman fishing with a couple of men this time, and he was amazed that she seemed to be enjoying herself more than the men were. It just goes to show you that you should never presume that things are just the same with all trips. Sometimes things just surprise you like that.

At eight thirty, she was ready for bed. There was only one trip out tomorrow, and then she'd be back by dinner time again. She loved being home at night every day and was happy that she had a job that she could get paid for doing such short trips. Most of the time, bigger companies wanted to pay you by the mile. Taylor was paying her weekly, and she was making good money, too. Enough that she was able to put a bit back weekly for house payments and such.

Getting the boxes broken down that were still in the garage, she had all the things that had been delivered put away. There were a few things that she'd ordered that had been for her rig, and she took them out to it so that she'd have it finished. With her rig enhanced like it was, she really didn't need all that much, but it was nice to have meals put in the freezer from Jack that she could just pick up and go with. She was looking forward to having a nice meal on the road, like her mom used to make them when she was riding with them.

At ten, she'd heard from Colby twice. The traffic out of the harbor was thick, and he wasn't able to just leave. Also, the people on the trip had had such a good time, they wanted to talk to him about booking another trip closer to the fall. He had room for one more trip, he told her, and that would have him booked up until the following year.

"I'm going to need the second boat before too much longer, the way things are going." She told him again that she was proud of him, and he told her that he loved her. The times he said that made her heart tingle. Smiling to herself, she told him that she loved him as well.

When he got home, she was so tired that she had been napping on the couch. It was after eleven, and he told her how sorry he was several times before she finally told him it was fine, that he was home now, and that she just wanted to go to bed.

Almost as soon as her head hit the pillow, she was out. When Colby joined her in the bed, she wrapped her arms around him and fell back to sleep. She knew on some level that she was going to sleep better tonight than she had in a long time. With a kiss to her forehead, Emma told Colby that she loved him and closed her eyes. It was too exhausting having a new home, she thought, and wondered if they might have been better off living in her truck. Sleep took her under quickly, and she couldn't believe that she was sleeping with Colby, finally, and was actually sleeping.

The next morning dawned bright and early, and she found herself alone in the big bed. Colby had left her a note that said that he'd be back for lunch. He'd gotten one of his brothers to cover for him for the rest of the day, but he had to work at the foundation today and had forgotten. Disappointment made her angry, and she stomped her way to the bathroom. They were never going to have sex at this rate.

They'd been sleeping together for one night, and neither of them was getting any younger. That made her laugh out loud in the bathroom as she thought that they were about as young as they were going to be forever because of the magic. Getting in a better mood, she thought of wearing a pretty sundress and was glad that the one that appeared on her was bright yellow with tiny little daisies all over it. With a nice pair of summer shoes, she was ready for the day. She really didn't have much to do today, but she was going to make the most of it.

Making arrangements for the last few things that

they needed to be delivered, she was about as bored as she'd been in a while. Not that she minded being bored, it was by far better than being stressed out with driving. And that made her think about whether she was enjoying driving as much as she did before.

She didn't know what she'd do with her free time, but the thought of getting in her rig and driving for hours again wasn't as appealing as it had been before. Nor did she like the long hours of solitude that went along with it. Thinking that she was going to have to talk to Taylor again before she went out again, she didn't want to leave them in a bind by not wanting to work anymore. She knew that she'd never be angry with her about it, but she was thinking that other than one or two days a week, she didn't want to drive all the time anymore.

She wanted to be home when Colby was. Or waiting for him to come home to be with her. Never one to think that she'd be at the beck and call of a man before, she wondered if it just had to do with waking up alone in the bed. That was more than likely it, she told herself. It wasn't that she wanted to be a housewife all the time. She didn't know if she'd like that any more than she did driving right now.

Time would tell, she supposed, and wanted to talk it over with Colby before she made any decisions concerning her job. The big question was, what would she do with herself all day if she didn't have anything to do?

Chapter 7

Taylor had taken Ivy with her to the reading of the will. She didn't want to be here, and didn't care who knew it. The attorney was an older man who looked like he'd rather be anyplace else but with her, too. She supposed it didn't help that she'd been sniping at him since she'd arrived. She had better things to do other than to sit around hearing from people that she didn't know or care enough about her to get to know her. As soon as the man, she'd forgotten his name twice now, got down to business, she understood a little more about what was going on with her mother, too.

"They wanted me to explain a few things to you, please, before we begin. They were an older couple when they had Gilda Jane. In their late forties by then, and they didn't expect to have any children of their own. You might say that they were, at the beginning very happy to have a healthy little girl to see them into their golden age." He cleared his throat before moving on. "Not to say that she did anything for her when she got older, but to make their lives a living hell. The child that she became was much worse than the adult that she eventually became."

"I don't understand. I was told that they pampered her every need, and that's why she was like she was. Thinking that the world revolved only because she was in it." He said that they had, but there was more. "More what then? I mean, they were feeling guilty about making her marry my dad, given the way that she was. What else could it be?"

"She killed two people by the time she was a teenager." She didn't know what to expect, but that would have been low on her list if at all. "They had to pay for her not to go to prison, and that was just the beginning of the trouble they had with her. They were forever paying to get her out of one thing or another. Millions of dollars were spent on getting her out of one thing or the next. In addition to the two deaths, there were numerous lawsuits brought against her because she didn't like not being the center of attention. As you well know about."

"She killed two people because she couldn't—why wasn't she in prison? I mean, most people would be because they killed someone." He said it was her mental capacity. "I still don't understand. Perhaps you should start at the beginning. That way, I can understand what she was about when she murdered two people and didn't spend any time in jail for."

"When she was born, she wasn't very healthy. They pampered her too much, even I saw that, but they were loving, too. They didn't just give her everything that she wanted, but they were able to afford to give her things just to keep her in line, too. A pony had been her third birthday gift. Then, when she was sixteen, they bought her a car. Things that most parents with a little bit of funding do for their kids." She nodded, waiting for him to get to the part where they left her in her father's care. "They never wanted her to marry and had even told your father that he shouldn't marry her. But they needed out. They were getting too old to handle her temper tantrums all the time. They even warned him not to have children with her."

"He never told my grandma that part. He said that they just got her married off to him and left him trying to get her to behave." He said there was much more than that to the entire story. "I'm assuming so now. Why did he want her to have a child when he'd been warned and probably lived with her for a time, knowing what she was like?"

"He told her that once the child was born, he'd take care of everything. He thought, and I can understand why he'd think this, that if she had someone who was dependent on her, she'd be less selfish about her own needs. She only got worse." It seemed to her that he was jumping all over the place when she simply wanted to understand what had happened. Asking him to start at the first part again, he nodded and handed her a file that had several sheets of paper in it. Taylor handed it off to Ivy so that she could get the man in gear to tell her what had happened.

"A man that she had seen in the grocery store told her to behave herself, that she was making a scene. She didn't like to be told no, as you well know, and she picked up a can of something and beat him nearly to death with it. He died later at the hospital. That was the first time that your grandparents paid for something that she'd done. They had her put into an asylum then, but she didn't last but a few days; they'd had enough of her and had them come and get her. The next time wasn't as bad, but the child that she'd been wanting to play with had wanted to go home, and she didn't want that. Gilda Jane killed him by pushing him into oncoming traffic, which resulted in the second time they had to pay." She didn't know what to think. Her mother was a murderer? This wasn't right. She should have been in prison—

"That's why she tells people that she's going to kill them. She'd gotten away with it twice as a child, and she thought that someone would just pay off whatever she'd done, and that's why she thought that I should just give her money. To shut people up." Taylor leaned back in her chair. "She really is a monster. And they knew it when they got her to marry my dad."

"Your father knew too. He was given a contract to sign telling him of all her misdeeds and horrific childhood." He handed her another file, and she again handed it off to Ivy. "I don't know the mind of your father, Mrs. Tucker, but I do know that he was well aware of things that had gone on before he'd married her. I don't know if he thought that he could change her or what, but he had a complete understanding of what kind of person she was before he wed her."

"Then I'm more confused than ever. It was said that she killed him off at a young age because of her demands on his life. That can't be true if he had knowledge of her before they were wed." He said that the only thing that came to mind was that he thought that he could change her somehow. "So he goes into their marriage with his eyes wide open and his heart thinking that he's better at changing someone with a mental disability like she had and thought that he could change her when nothing else worked. I'm assuming that there had been doctors' appointments with professionals, too."

"More than a dozen. When it was obvious that nothing was going to work, they gave up, gave her what she wanted, and when your father came along to marry her, they made sure that he knew what he was getting into. After the wedding, your grandparents hid from your father more than they did their daughter simply because they thought that he'd divorce her after a time and they'd be stuck with her again." Taylor didn't know what to think, so she just sat there. Of course, he could tell her anything that he wanted, and there was no one to dispute his word, but the contract that her father had signed was proof that he knew something was going on with her mom. "Are you ready to hear what else they left you? I know that they knew that your father had died and that you were born. They kept close tabs on you, too. Knowing that you had your great-grandmother around soothed them in some ways."

"Soothed them? Who was there to soothe me when she was demanding all my time? Who was there for me when she told me that she'd kill a child that I had simply because she wanted all the attention on herself? No one was there." Ivy simply put her hand on her arm, and she calmed down a bit. "I don't know that I want to know what they left me. The money to me was dirty enough. But this? This feels like they're trying to buy me off with the will and whatever it says."

"I would imagine that's exactly what they're doing." She was startled by his saying that and stared at him. "They had no qualms about telling people what they'd done. In fact, they were shunned in most places they lived because they'd abandoned you in fear of their daughter. When they approached my firm with wanting to get their will taken care of, they were turned away at first. Then, of course, there was the money involved. The firm that I worked for was forever doing things because of the money involved in things. So your grandparents were no different in wanting things taken care of so that they could die without any fears of being guilty of any of their past deeds. I almost didn't want to do it myself, but I was given a bonus just to do it."

"I'm sorry." She was, too. None of this was his fault. She was thinking that her best move would be to let him read the will and take what was given to her and move on. Just because it had been something they wanted her to have, she didn't have to take it. She could do just what she'd done with the money, give it away and not have to worry about it again. "If you'd not mind reading the will, I can leave you to the rest of your day and whatever you have planned."

"Thank you." He picked up the blue folder and began to read from it. There was nothing she could do about what was being said, so she zoned out. Thinking instead of the will of grandparents that she didn't know to the things she had going on at work. Thinking that whatever was going on there was by far better than anything going on here. She also knew that if there was something that she needed to pay attention to, Ivy would poke her in the ribs or something so that she could focus on it.

She had been asked from another distribution center if she could handle a few more stores. They were having delivery issues and wanted her to deliver their products along with what she had already. It was something that she never considered when she'd opened her own distribution center. She was sure she could make it work, but did she want to? It would mean more work for her drivers and employees at the center, but would it be worth the trouble of printing up the labels for the stores and having trucks make an extra few stops on their already busy schedule? She'd only just gotten her drivers up to speed and had hired enough of them. Now she was thinking about hiring more. What to do, what to do.

Then there was the fact that she was going to see how she could get pregnant. She knew how to get that way, but she was waiting for the timing of it. She couldn't wait to have a child with Jack. They were really busy now, and she was excited to see how busy they got with children around.

They were going to know that they were loved and she'd never treat them like her mother had treated her. Never. Also, she wouldn't give them everything in the world just because she could. There wasn't any way that she was going to spoil them so much that they thought they were better than anyone else. She wanted grounded children, ones that she could be proud of when she took them out in public. Taylor never wanted to take her mother out in public because of the way she acted. And she would cause a scene whenever they were out, especially when things didn't go her way.

When the attorney stood up, she did as well. While she had no idea what was going on, he would never know that. Asking for a few minutes alone with Ivy, she sat down when the other woman did, and she smiled at her. Ivy seemed to understand that she'd not been paying attention.

"They left you four houses that they use as rentals that are all over the world. There are two more insurance policies that are worth about two million dollars. They also donated a great deal of money to their favorite charity. But you're getting the bulk of it." She asked her how much and if there were any stipulations on the money. "None that he mentioned, but there is a letter for you again. Basically, it says again how sorry they were for dropping this all on you and hoped that someday you could forgive them. I'm sure you'll want to know after all these findings that you've been told about your father. I'm sorry to say, but he doesn't strike me as a man who should have been complaining about his lot in life when he was very aware of what was going on in the beginning."

"I don't feel sorry for any of them if you want the truth. They all played a part in my mother's behavior and should be punished for their parts in it. Including my dad." Ivy nodded. "You don't agree with me?"

"I do as a matter of fact. None of them was as innocent as they made themselves out to be. My question is, do you tell your grandma? She had been feeling guilty about her supposed part in this, too, I guess." She said she'd tell her simply because of that. "Good for you. She needs to know simply because she played no part in his being with your mother, not the way she feels like she does."

"I'll sit her down and show her what I got from this when she returns. I won't even hint about it while she's on vacation. I think that it's been waiting for me to find out after all this time, a few more days isn't going to matter a great deal." Ivy agreed with her and handed her the deeds to the house. "I'm assuming that I'm going to have to do something with this stuff, too, right?"

"I was thinking about the houses. You should keep them. If only for the reason that you can rent them out during the summer breaks, or even let it be a vacation spot for the family when they want to get away. One of them is in the south of France, and from what I read, it's a very nice house too. Large with four bedrooms. That would be a great place to go to unwind." She asked her if she wanted it. "I don't even own a passport, much less the time to go to someplace like that. It would be magical, but I can't afford to go with a baby coming along."

"I'm going to do as you said and make it a vacation home for the family." Ivy nodded then laughed. "Now what's funny? You want to go, too, don't you? Well, you're going to be the first person to use it. Before the baby comes along. It will be just what you and Hudson need. A vacation in France."

Ivy didn't say anything more about it, but Taylor was going to make it happen. She was the best attorney she'd ever had, and she was going to make sure that she knew how much she was appreciated. Even Ronin was singing her praises.

After gathering things up that she'd need, Taylor made her way home. Today, she was going to spend the day in the garden to reset and balance her life. If nothing else, they'd have fresh garden vegetables for dinner. And that alone would make it worthwhile for her to walk around the yard in her bare feet. She so loved summer and the things that they had on the estate. But she also couldn't wait for her grandma to get home so she could hang out with her. She'd not had a good lunch date in a month. Taylor decided to invite the other women to go with her and have some fun. Then she'd not miss her grandma so much.

~*~

Colby was trying to think of a way to seduce his wife. Not that it would take all that much effort on his part, she'd been telling him for days that she wanted him, but things were getting in the way all the time, and he wanted to be with her. Being at home alone made him realize how much he'd been away from the house of late and was missing her a great deal. And the things going on around the home.

Yesterday, he'd noticed that they had a butler. His name was Chance, and he was about as stiff as a board when it came to joking around with him. He said that he'd think his jokes were funny when he was off duty. How was that to happen? But he stopped joking around with the man and went about his day.

Then there were the domestics. He hated calling them that, but it was the only name they had for what they did around the house. And since they didn't wear name tags, something that he only just noticed, too, he didn't have a name to call them either. This living in the fancy life wasn't all that friendly feeling to him. Colby was in the living room when Emma finally came home.

"I've missed you." She kissed him on the mouth, and he pulled her back in for another kiss. "I've really missed you. I'm off tomorrow as Douglas is going to take the boat out tomorrow on his own for the first time."

"I don't have to be to work until after two. I have a short run and then I'm off for the next two days. But I do have to work the weekend." Their schedules were forever crossed. "I'm thinking about stopping driving so much and going down to one or two days a week. I miss too much about having you around."

"With Douglas going on runs of his own, I might put off buying another boat until he feels comfortable with it. That way, when he takes out more and more, I'll be home to be with you." She told him she liked that idea, then asked him what he thought about her dropping her full-time status. "I think that's the only way we're going to be able to see each other, is if we both take a few days off together and get to know how the other half of my family lives. Did I tell you that Taylor is going to find someone to run her businesses for her? Jack is training someone to take some of the dinners off his hands, and he'll work only on the weekend. I think they're feeling the same as we are. Pressure from both halves working all the time."

They sat on the couch until dinner and talked about what it would be like not working full-time. She said that she'd have to find something to do during the day so that she could feel productive. But he pointed out that she could work at the foundation that much and still be a part of the family business when they needed her.

"I like that idea. I could still be a part of the business and not have to be out on the road all the time. It'll be perfect. But she had to talk with Taylor before she started getting into a new job. The woman had been wonderful to them, and there was no way she was going to make Taylor upset with her. She asked Colby if she thought that she'd be mad.

"I don't. Like I said, she's thinking of slowing down as well. I think at some point all of us will be doing that. I've noticed that Denver and Bailee have done the same thing now that they're the head of the leap." She said there was that. "Of course, Lance and Georgie are still working a great deal, but the rest of us aren't."

After dinner, they went out to the deck to check on the hot tub. It had been filled the morning before, so it was nice and hot, ready to be used tonight. After making sure that they were alone, the two of them stripped down to their skin and got into it. They sat on either side of the tub, not looking at one another.

"I was just thinking about how my body isn't all that much to look at." He asked her what she was talking about. "You've seen me. I have barely any boobs, and my hips are so wide from sitting on my ass all day. I wonder if I'll be able to lose that when I start exercising again."

Colby moved to sit next to her. "I see nothing at all wrong with your body. It's perfect. She scoffed at him. "You aren't allowed to say anything negative about your body again. I know perfection when I see it. You have beautiful breasts and wonderful hips. I'd love to hang onto them while I'm pounding you from behind."

"Really?" She rolled to her front and stood up, holding onto the side of the tub. "You mean like this? I think that would be a wonderful way to break in the tub, don't you? I mean, no one will hear us out here. What do you think?"

Instead of answering her, he stood up behind her. Without any forethought as to what she might be feeling, he slammed his cock into her pussy from behind, which had her crying out. It was perfect as they'd been working up to this point all week, and foreplay had been everything they'd done. Not in pain, but the most incredible pleasure she'd had in a very long time.

"Is this what you wanted?" She nodded and lowered her head so that it touched the side of the tub. "That's it, baby. Give me everything that you have."

Colby reached around her back and cupped her breasts in his hand. Squeezing her nipples and fucking her hard, she felt a climax rolling up her legs to her core. When he slid one of his fingers into her with his cock, she cried out again with a release that was so profound that she was sure that she blacked out for a moment.

"Steady now. I have you." He continued to fuck her like this as she stood in front of him. When he asked her to turn around, turning her so quickly that she nearly fell, she was sitting on the side of the tub, where he grinned at her. "I'm going to feast on you. Then I'm going to lay you out and fuck you until neither one can stand."

"Yes, please." Once she was seated on the side, he knelt down in the water until just his face was there. Watching him as he eyed her pussy, she felt herself weep with a wetness that somewhat embarrassed her. "I'm so wet, Colby. Like I've been bathed in my cum."

"Oh baby, that's what I want to hear." He leaned in and licked her pussy before blowing his breath over her. She felt her toes curl tightly as he leaned in closer and licked her again. When he slid his finger into her, she nearly came up off the side of the tub until he started fucking her like that. Christ, she wanted to come so badly that her ears were ringing loudly.

Between fucking her and eating her, she lost track of how many times she came. All she knew was that her body belonged to Colby and that he could do whatever he wanted to her and she'd love it. Standing up, she nearly begged him to finish her when he slid his cock into her sheath. He didn't move but to throw back his head and close his eyes. When he looked at her, she could see the lion that he was as it moved over his skin, and she shivered at the thought of him loving her as well.

Leaning over her again, he took her breasts into his mouth and suckled hard while he fucked her. Her nipples were beyond hard and painful, but she didn't care. She was getting the fucking of her life and she was going to enjoy every bit of it.

"Come for me, love." She wrapped her legs around his hips and felt his cock go deeper still. "That's it, love. That's what I want. To feel you wrapped around my cock like you're never going to let it go."

Colby fucked her slowly, going in and out of her like it was going to go on forever. And a large part of her wanted it to, but she needed more from him. Something so epic that her body and mind would never be the same afterwards.

When he cupped her ass, bringing her closer to him, it was all she could do to hang onto his shoulders. Even when he started to take her harder, faster, she dug her nails into his shoulders so that she'd not fly away. And for whatever reason, she thought that when she came, she was going to come apart in so many pieces that she'd never find them all again, and she'd only be a part of a whole. She'd be a whole woman because of the way he was taking her.

"Come." The command ripped through her, and she screamed. Needing something else to hold onto, she leaned upward and sank her teeth into his neck. The taste of his coppery blood had her crying out more until she had nothing left in her and let go. Knowing that Colby would catch her no matter what, she sank into unconsciousness like she was falling asleep in her bed.

Waking up, she was in her bed and wondered why she didn't wake up when she was brought up here. Then her skin began to crawl like it was on fire, and she sat up in bed. Colby was coming out of the bathroom when she felt her skin turn inside out. Christ, it was magic or torture, she didn't know what, but she was going to die from it and soon.

"I have you, baby." She nodded, still hurting from whatever was going on with her. "It'll be over in a minute.

It's just a bit more magic."

"How do you know?" He said he'd gotten the same, but she was getting a bit more because she didn't have as much as he did. "I don't want it. It hurts."

"I'm so sorry. I really am." She was starting to feel a little better after a few more minutes, and she asked if he'd been hurt too. "Not so much as you. As soon as it rolled over me, I knew it was going to be painful for you, honey. I'm so sorry. I should have warned you about it."

"How could you have known?" She was almost over it, and her body was protesting, her muscles aching again. "I just got my shoulder to be all right, now I'm hurting again. Will this ever be stopped?"

Colby laughed, and she glared at him. "I'm sorry, but you have to admit that it wasn't as bad as it could have been. You're going to be just fine now. You'll figure out your magic and you'll not believe how good you'll feel after today—or tonight, I don't know what time it is." She could see the clock across the room and didn't know what time it was either. It was like it was all blurry. "How are you feeling? I was just filling the tub with some hot water for you. I guess we could have stayed in the hot tub for a while more, but it was getting chilly out, and this was the only place I could think we could rest. Are you better now?"

"I am." She moved to her back and wished for her warm PJs on. Once she was warmed up, she did feel a good deal better. "I'd like to soak in the tub for a while. I have a feeling that I'm going to be sore in the morning too."

"Maybe not. You're not sore now, are you?" She told him that she was thinking that she felt better all the way around. "Good. Maybe we can get you in the tub and then sleep in tomorrow. I know neither of us has to be to work until later in the afternoon. What do you say to that?"

She was just slipping into the tub when she moaned. It did feel better to be in the warm water, and she wondered how soon she'd feel back to normal. Her mind was buzzing with the new magic she supposed, and she wasn't sure what some of it was.

Like before, she knew that having Colby by her side would work wonders for her overwrought mind, and she'd just lean on him. Closing her eyes, she was happy to have had him in her life right now. Life was suddenly really good for her.

Chapter 8

Kayce wasn't sure what was going on in his office building, but there was something. The doctors weren't very close at all, and they seemed to be avoiding one another. Him too, but he didn't care. He wasn't close to anyone he worked with. Just as he was going into one of the rooms that were set up for him, he was stopped by his nurse.

"I'm going to go in with you." Kayce told her that wasn't necessary. "Yes, it is. I'll go in with you so that you're safe. Just don't tell me to leave you unless you leave first. Understand?"

"No. But I'll do what you tell me." He opened the door and saw a flash of red. The woman who was being seated on the room's chair was wearing a dress so bright red that it hurt his eyes. Then he noticed what the dress consisted of. Holy Christ, she might well have been naked for all it covered on her body. He'd seen more material on a bathing suit; this was so tight and skimpy.

"There you are." She had a pinched look on her face. "You doctors always have a woman around you. It's almost like you don't trust us to be in the same room together."

He didn't. In that moment, he didn't trust her as far as he could toss her. And being a lion and healthy, he figured he could toss her pretty far. As soon as he looked at the chart, then at the little boy who was seated on the table for him, he moved around the woman and looked at the child.

"I have paperwork that tells me that you fell at school today, Tim. Can you tell me what you were doing when you fell?" The woman said that she would answer the questions. "All right, but I'm going to need his side of the story first. Then you can tell me your version of what happened."

"He was playing on the swing when he fell out." Tim said that he had jumped out and had fallen on the rocks. "Okay, he jumped out. I thought someone said that he was pushed out of the swing. Can you get your girl here to go and get me a box of tissues? I'm feeling very emotional right now."

"There's a box — well, there was a box on the counter. No worries, I can get you a box right here." He was never so glad that they stocked tissues in the rooms for usage. "There you go. Now, Tim, where did you get hurt? Your knees or your arms?" Putting them on the counter, he saw the previous box in the trash can. So that had been what she'd been doing when she had been moving around in the room.

"I didn't get hurt at all. I was having fun when they called my mom in." Kayce didn't understand what was going on with the school if they called the mother in for no reason, but that wasn't why he was here. He was going to examine the little boy and make sure that nothing was broken. Ignoring the mother, whom he assumed was the mother of Tim, he examined his knees and his wrists before getting to his elbows. "I guess I did get them all scuffed up. They don't hurt like they did at the school nurse's room."

"There are stones still in the wounds. How about we clean them up and get the stones and grass out of them before we bandage them up for you?" Tim was all for it, and that was when he noticed that the mom was talking to his nurse. Abby wasn't having anything to do with her trying to send her out of the room. "We'll need a clean-up kit for Tim, and I'll go and get it. If you could call the school for me, Abby, we can get to the bottom of why the wounds weren't cleaned at the school. They should have made some sort of effort to clean them up."

"Why can't she just get the kit or whatever and call the school at the same time? Why do you need her in here in the first place?" He said that he always had a nurse in with him, and he liked it that way. "Well, I don't. It's too crowded in here with all four of us. Why can't it just be the two of us? And Tim, of course?"

Kayce left the room first and went down the hall to get the kit. While Abby was on the phone, he stood waiting for her to get finished with the phone call. There wasn't any way he was going back in that room alone. The woman had claws that were far-reaching, and he wasn't going to be a part of whatever she had in mind.

He wasn't stupid in thinking that he didn't have a clue. He just didn't want to think that someone like her would get him tricked into whatever she had going on in her head. Now he understood why the other doctors were avoiding him. They wanted no part of—the least they could have done was warn him what was going on.

The sooner he got out of this practice, the better he'd like it. There was no friendship around here. They didn't do anything after work. It was as if they were all on their own and didn't want anything to do with the rest of them. He'd had enough. The one time he'd tried to get to know his fellow doctors, he was told that they didn't socialize, they just worked together, and nothing more. It wasn't what he wanted in a practice at all.

When Abby got off the phone, she told him that the school had orders not to clean up anything about Ms. Jacobson's son. If he was sick, they were to let him vomit, then call her. Nothing was to be done with her child, and they were to call her when something happened. She would take him to the doctor when she saw fit. Apparently, even when he wasn't ill, she'd take him out of school to run him to the doctor just to get a second opinion.

"You knew this?" Abby said she was sorry, but everyone knew about Ms. Jacobson. "I see. Well, I guess I'm happy that you didn't abandon me when you had the chance. Let's get this over with and move on. In the future, I'd appreciate a heads up about what is going on."

"Yes, sir." She paused for about a minute before she spoke again. "She's looking for a man to sue. She wants to get you into a room alone so that she can say that you made a pass at her. She's tried it before, but all the doctors here are aware of her ways and are never alone with her. She'll sue you for sexual assault."

"And everyone knows this but allows her to come here." Abby nodded even though it wasn't a question.

"And they knew that she was making an appointment with me this morning."

"They switched their schedules around so that you'd get her today. I don't know that they were hoping that I'd not say anything, but we nurses stick together even if our bosses don't." Kayce decided that he was going to give Abby the heave-ho when he left this place. He didn't want tricks and half-truths when it came to working together. He had to trust her, and right now he didn't. Even though she'd told him eventually, it could have been bad had she not. She put her hand on his arm. "Are you mad at me? I did tell you."

"Yes, I'm furious with you. This could have been really bad for me." He opened the door and made his way in, hoping that Abby would come in with him. "All right, Tim. Let's get you cleaned up."

Abby did come in with him and helped him clean up the wounds on Tim's elbows. Once he was wrapped up, he gave instructions to the mother to make sure he kept his wounds clean, and he could take the bandage off tomorrow. Just as they were leaving, Ms. Jacobson put her arm on his.

"We could have a good time the two of us." He told her to unhand him. When she didn't move her hand off of him, he let just a little of his cat go to show her he wasn't a pushover. She leapt back so quickly she nearly fell off her heels. Good. Maybe she'd leave him alone from now on. "You're not right. This isn't going the way it usually does. I want a different doctor."

"I can do that for you; however, no one is going to

be left in the room with you alone, not even with your son. You might as well find yourself another doctor's office to try your tricks with. It will no longer work here." He was just angry enough to tell her off, but he had to remain calm. Right now, his lion wanted out to teach her a lesson, and he was barely controlling him. "You have a good day, Ms. Jacobson, and take my advice on this office."

For the rest of the day, Abby was a model nurse. She never left him alone in any of the patients' rooms, nor did she mention Ms. Jacobson again. By the end of his day, he was exhausted and had a headache, something that he'd never had before. Stress, he knew what it was, and thought that he knew what it was from. Trying to keep a good front for all his other patients was taking its toll on him.

After work, he did something that he'd never done before. He stopped at the pizza place that had beer and sat down at the booth. Ordering himself a beer and a large pizza, he was sitting there waiting on both when his brother Lance walked in. He sat in the booth with him and smiled.

"Georgie said she talked to Abby this morning. Said you were having a shitty day." He told him to go away. "I won't do that if you think to drown yourself in beer all night. Come home with me, we'll share our combined pizza orders and have a good time."

"She knew what was going on. She wasn't going to—what do you mean, Georgie spoke to Abby? Since when are they friends?" He told him what had happened. "So she called to talk to me and got Abby instead. That's a breach of some kind of professionalism, don't you think?"

"Abby was worried that you were going to fire her and talked to Georgie when she called. I'd call it like you did. A breach, but she was worried and thought that Georgie was a friend and not a family member." He still didn't care for it. "Neither do I. But it's done now, and you're coming home with me. For dinner."

"I just want to be left alone. I've not had a moment's peace since she showed up this morning and started my day off with her ways. Did you hear what she was wearing? Who wears that sort of dress to a doctor's office with their kid? No one that's who. Christ, I've had a really crappy day, and I don't know that it could get any worse." He told him not to say that or the fates would take it as a challenge. "That would be just what I need, my mate to show up about now and demand something of me. I might be the last one to get a mate, but I'm certainly not in the mood for one. I've seen the way they twist you up in a knot and hang you out to dry."

"That was all on us, not our mates." He just shook his head when his beer was brought to him. "Can you bring him a bottle of water, too? He's changed his mind about the beer. Haven't you, Kayce?"

He thought about drinking it anyway, but he really didn't want it. Nodding that he was right, he glared at his older brother. There were times when he hated being the youngest, and it mattered little that he was old enough to vote and be a doctor. He would forever be the baby in their eyes, no matter how old he got.

While they were boxing up his pizza with his

brother's order, they made their way to his home. Lance was going to pick him up and take him to their home, but he wanted to change out of his scrubs, something that he wore to work daily, and put on some nicer clothing. As he was coming out of his house in favor of going to Lance and Georgie's, his house phone rang.

"Doctor Tucker? This is the switchboard for the firm that you work with. There has been an emergency going on at the hospital with one of your patients. Mr. Toby has had a fall and would like you to be there with him." He said that he wasn't on call, but he'd go to see him. "Thank you, sir. The doctor on duty tonight said to give you a call since Mr. Toby is one of yours."

That's not how being on call worked, but he didn't say anything to her. Instead, he grabbed a slice of pizza and went back to change clothes again. He knew Mr. Toby was an elderly man in his late eighties and worried for him. Even though he was a pediatrician, he had treated the man while in med school, and he had been calling him in every time he was in the hospital. He was the only person over thirteen that he saw, and he loved the elderly gentleman.

Getting to the hospital, Kayce wasn't surprised to find him in the emergency department. He'd taken a tumble, he'd been told, and had banged up his leg and head. The man was a mess when he was able to see him. Taking the elderly man's hand into his, he wasn't happy with the weakness of his grip.

"I told you about those steps, didn't I?" He said that he was showing off to his granddaughter. "See what that got you? A messed-up head trauma and a banged-up knee. What am I going to do with you?"

"Roll me into a grave and be done with me." He said he'd never do that; he was his best patient. "Best or not, I'm afraid I've done myself in this time. Hurt myself bad." He said he'd order some tests after examining him. "My granddaughter would have my head if she weren't so worried about me. Durn near ran her down when I was falling, too."

Mr. Toby started crying, and it tore at his heart. Waiting for him to regain his composure, he held his hand, checking his pulse while he was at it. Even for as upset as he was, his heart rate was a little slow. Instead of asking about the fall, which he could tell had taken a great deal out of Mr. Toby, he asked about his granddaughter.

"She's a might mad at me right now, you understand. I know you are, too. But she's come to visit me for a week and I had to go and fall down like a durned old fool." Kayce examined Mr. Toby and declared that he did indeed need some tests run. In addition to a CT scan, he wanted him to have some bloodwork done as well. "She'll be around here soon. My Molly had to park the car someplace and then come in."

"I'm going to start on the tests now, Mr. Toby. That way, we can get some answers about why you fell." After asking him a series of questions, he said that he had blacked out a little bit when he'd hit his head. That wasn't what he wanted to hear about him, so he ordered a couple of more tests to be run. "I'll talk to someone when you get back. All right. Is your granddaughter old enough to get information about your health?"

"She's darn near twenty-five years old, so I'd guess she is." He didn't make a joke about her age, but had said it like it was a question whether or not she was. Kayce said that he'd talk to her and him when he got back from the tests. He was being wheeled out of the room for the first set of tests to be run, just as someone came into it. Kayce paused long enough to tell the young woman that he was headed for tests and would be back shortly. Then he went to put in the orders that would get Mr. Toby to feeling better.

~*~

Molly was frantically worried about her Pop-Pop. Seeing him fall down the stairs like he had, had aged her fifty years, she thought. Then, when she'd called for an ambulance, he'd told her that he wanted to die. That he was just too old to be around anymore. It broke her heart that he thought that way, and she didn't know what to do about it.

She paced the little room he'd been in while he was gone getting tests run, and wondered what she'd do without him around anymore. It had been something that she'd been thinking about forever. He was all she had in the world and didn't want to lose him just yet.

But he was in his eighties, and she knew that the fact that he'd made it this long was a miracle. He'd lost his wife when they'd been in their fifties, and it broke her heart that Grannie wasn't around, too. But to lose him now would be devastating to her. There was no one else that she cared for as much as she did the old man.

Her father was around, she supposed, but she didn't care for him at all. Then there were her two brothers, who were younger than her. Seth and Ryan were a pain in her ass whenever they were around, and she couldn't stand them either. Since she'd gotten older and was now in the service, they didn't bother her so much now, but her father did, and that was about as bad as it got, she thought.

She'd been on leave since yesterday, and then her Pop-Pop had fallen today. The poor old man had beaten himself up, too. Molly had ten more days to stay in town before she had to leave again, and she knew she was going to miss visiting with her Pop-Pop unless she stayed in the hospital with him. She loved him very much.

"Miss, I was asked to tell you to go and get you something to eat as Mr. Toby is going to be a little while longer." She said she'd wait for him. "All right, but it might be another hour before he gets his scan. They're backed up a great deal."

"Thank you for telling me. I'll wait for him. I don't want him to think that he can fob me off so quickly as sending me to get something to eat. I have an idea he meant for me to go home and not to return." The nurse laughed and said that was what he'd said too. "I thought as much. He can be a stinker when he wants to be."

Molly only had about six months until she was getting out of the service. She'd done her time so that she could get a college education and then be able to better herself. Her plan had been to become a doctor, but the thought of being a nurse appealed to her more. She didn't want the stuffiness of becoming what some doctors did when they got out of college.

When her Pop-Pop returned, he was a little groggy. Asking him what he'd been given didn't help her any, so she waited for someone to come and tell her. That was another long wait while Pop-Pop dozed off and on for the next couple of hours. They did come and check on him a couple of times, but they were waiting on the doctor to tell them what to do next.

Finally showing up, the doctor looked like he'd taken a good one to the face. His nose had been bleeding, there was still a bit of blood on his nose, and his lip had two stitches in it. She asked him what had happened, and he just looked at her like she was some kind of germ under a microscope. Molly wanted to hit him again.

"I fell into someone's fist." She asked him how that had happened, and he didn't look like he wanted to tell her. "A combative patient came in, and they thought that I'd have better luck at holding him down until they could get some medication into his system."

"That sounds dangerous. Why would they think you'd be able to do that when they have bigger men working here?" She really didn't care but was curious enough to ask questions to keep her nerves from taking over, worrying about her Pop-Pop. "I mean, you're in good shape and all, but you don't strike me as a man who likes to get too involved in what his patients want from him."

"What the hell does that mean?" She shrugged and said her Pop-Pop had been waiting for him for over three hours now. "And I told you I was asked to help out with someone else. Or would you have rather he'd gotten away from the police and gone on a rampage around the hospital killing whomever he came in contact with? That would include your Pop-Pop, too."

"I didn't know that." He said that she should never assume anything about him when it came to his job. "I'm sorry, and you're right. I shouldn't have thought that you were out fucking around while my Pop-Pop was suffering. Though it looks like someone gave him something for pain. Did you do that?"

He didn't answer her but did talk to her grandfather. Pop-Pop was still groggy, but he was able to answer the questions that the doctor put to him. As he laid there, she could tell then that he was getting treatment. The doctor was also kind and calm with him, nothing like he'd been with her. Not that she didn't deserve it, she'd been nasty with him, but she was worried, and he should have taken that into consideration.

"You have a concussion, Mr. Toby. And you've bruised your ankle. I want you to stay here for a couple of days to make sure that you can get the medication you need. Also, we'll be able to keep a good eye on those cuts you have on your head while we're at it." Pop-Pop told him that he'd be fine when he got home, as his granddaughter was there now. "I'd rather you stay with us for those two days just to keep an eye on you. I'd hate to have sent you home, and you have to come back because of some kind of infection or something worse."

"What do you think, Molly? You didn't come to see me while I was in the hospital, now did you? Would you do this old man a favor and come see me while I'm in here?" She said, of course, she would; he was the reason she was home in the first place. "All right then, doc. I'll stay here, and I promise not to make too much of a fuss because I'm missing time with my girl here. She's all I've got myself in the whole world since my missus has passed on."

"Pop-Pop, you have a son and two grandsons. What if they were to show up and want to see you? What would you do?" He said he'd tell them to go home. "Well, I would, too, I guess. They don't have a great deal to do with you. But they are a part of your family."

"True." They put him in a room with a bigger bed. Pop-Pop wasn't a big man, but he did like to spread out when he was in pain. She got a good look at his ankle while they were moving him and couldn't believe that he hadn't broken it.

It was bruised from the side of his foot all the way up to his knee. There were scratches, too, on it that looked to her like he could have used a few stitches. The top of his foot looked the worst with a bruise that went from his ankle to his toes and had bruised them up as well. Poor man, her heart hurt for him. The doctor came in just as the transporters had him settled in the bed.

"You can have something to eat if you want, Mr. Toby. I'm not going to change your diet, but keep you on the one that I suggested several months ago. Are you still trying to cut out your salt? I've noticed that your legs aren't swollen like they usually are." She wanted to tell the doctor that he'd follow the plan if she had anything to do with it, but her grandfather said he was following it the best he could. "That's all we can hope for right now. You rest up, and in a couple of days, we'll have a look at your head again. I don't see anything coming of it, but you took a nasty fall, and I would like for you to be around for a few more years if you do all right."

When he asked for something for his headache, she could see where he might need something more. And when the doctor suggested that he take the heavier drugs while he could — so he could rest better — Molly wanted to tell them she'd take care of him if it came to that. She had something in her purse that helped with her headaches, and she would have offered it to him had he just asked. But then she realized that might not be such a good thing, not with him being in the hospital for his injuries. The medication that they gave him knocked him out, and she was sort of glad for it. She didn't want to see him in any pain.

The nurses said he would more than likely sleep through the night, and she was going to stay with him. One of them brought her a pillow and blanket and showed her how to make the chair into a long bed. Moving it as close to his bed as she could and still touch his hand, she tried her best to sleep while he did.

Every time he moved, she would wake up. Even if he only moved his hands from hers, she would stand up and watch over him until he settled again. The nurses were really nice throughout the night, and she would talk to them when they came in to wake him up to get his blood pressure. Molly was happy that it stayed down where it was while he was sleeping.

Never knowing what she was going to be up to while home, she always had an extra pair of panties in her bag. When she was told she could use Pop-Pop's shower, she leapt at the chance to do so. The water was perfect, and she felt so much better than she did when she woke up. Just being able to wash her face and hair made her feel like a new person. Sitting in the room brushing her hair, glad that she was at least that prepared to be cleaned up, she watched her grandfather as he flirted with the nurses. He'd been that way even before her grannie had died, and she knew that it was as harmless as anything else he did.

"Doctor Tucker said to make sure you had something to eat. I can bring another breakfast in if you tell them what you want." She was shown how to order herself something to eat and was happy when she got it. "There is a soda machine right outside the nurses' station, and you can get things from there as well. Just let us know if you need anything else."

Pop-Pop was sore this morning, the doctor said he might be. Given something for the pain had him dozing some, but he was alert when she spoke to him. She was never so happy to have the nurses tell her that he was doing so much better than they thought that he would, what with the fall and his age factoring in. Molly was thrilled that he had not broken anything like a hip or his ankle when he'd fallen. She would remember that fall for the rest of her life.

Chapter 9

Colby was worried about his little brother. Kayce had taken a beating yesterday, and his nose had been broken along with other bruises that he had on his body. All he needed to do was to shift, and that would take care of them. But they had to have him wait on that, as there might be repercussions coming his way when there was a police report filed. The other man had been high on cocaine and had denied treatment for himself, but since the police had brought him in, it seemed that his opinion whether he lived or died wasn't part of his deal.

Kayce was in better shape than he was. He ran ten miles every day and used the gym's punching bag three days a week. He said that he needed to be in shape because he had a practice to run, but they all thought it was because he was taking his aggressions out on the bag. Everyone knew that he hated where he worked.

Not that he could blame him. It was a hostile place to work, with everyone so tense all the time. It seemed to him that none of the doctors liked working there, as they wanted out like his brother did. But they'd helped him pave the way to get his student loans paid off, and he had another five months to work for the firm before he could even consider leaving.

"Why didn't you get help and be out on your own

when Ronin was setting us up with jobs and such?" He said that he thought that working for a practice like he was, he'd make some friends and not have to be on call all the time. "What can you do to opt out earlier? I mean, can you buy your contract from them? At least pay some of it off so that you don't have to remain there for so long?"

"I can buy out my contract, but it's really pricy. I only have a few months to go, then I can be out of it. I'd rather do it this way so that I can feel good about myself by not quitting halfway through it." Colby pointed out that he was miserable. "I am, this will make me appreciate being on my own better. And I will be and soon, but for now I'm working a job I got myself into through no fault of anyone else's but my own."

He tried talking him into something, anything. He even offered to lend him the money so that he could get out of it. They still had money left over from what Taylor had given them to fill out their home, but he wouldn't hear of it. He said he'd gotten himself into this and was going to get himself out of it, too.

To see him limping around and being in pain hurt him. He understood why he couldn't shift and make himself better, but he didn't have to like it. He would heal faster, but not fast enough for Colby. He didn't like pain himself, so hated it on one of his family.

"Your house looks great." He thought it did too and was glad that Kayce was going to be spending time with them over the next couple of days until he was moving around better. There were stairs in his place, a condo with a second floor, and he wasn't doing well enough to climb them nightly to go to his bedroom. They had two bedrooms on the first floor, and he hoped that his brother would enjoy one of them. "I've been looking at them too. I'm sick of living in my condo. I want to be able to stretch out like the rest of you can."

"I showed Emma my cat last night. She was very happy that I'm not as big as Ronin or Denver. I wanted to make sure that she could see all our lions so she could tell us apart, but everyone was busy. We'll get to it." Kayce said she'd have to wait to see his. "I know. I wish you could just get it over with and show her to heal, but I understand the reason why."

"It won't be much longer. A few days. I've had to have one of the others take over for a patient that I have in the hospital right now. And they're going to keep on top of my appointments that I can't keep right now." He asked him what had happened that made him have to hold down a patient. "Don't tell anyone else, but I was the only shifter in the room when he pulled out a gun. He later said that he was going to use it on himself and not us, but at the time, all I could think of was that he had a gun. The hospital is covering my costs for being out because I was helpful to the nurses in the room with him. He could have caused some serious damage to anyone who would have been around had he decided that he was going to get going with the gun. Christ, I've never been so afraid afterwards than I was at that moment."

"I bet. I would have done the same thing, I think. Better to be fast and have to apologize than to be slow and have to tell someone's family what happened." He then told him about what had happened at the office today. "Holy shit, buddy, you've had a shitty day. Why don't you tell me what your favorite meal is, and we'll have it tonight? Even if we have to order out. There is a great Chinese restaurant that delivers. We can get that."

"That sounds wonderful. I'll even pay for it." He told him that wasn't necessary, and they looked over the menu to see what he wanted. "And if you can get me about a gallon of hot and sour soup, I'll think I've gone to heaven."

By the time Emma got home, they were ready to eat. Leaving his brother at home, he went to pick up the food and drinks while Emma pulled into the driveway. They'd had Chinese just a few nights ago, but he could eat it all the time; he loved the food so much. And it was good to share such a meal with him when he could with his family.

They pigged out on the food with very few leftovers. That was fine with him as he could get it anytime he wished. Kayce was moving around a little better after getting his belly full, and he even said he felt better. That made it all worthwhile to him to have to give up the little bit of leftovers to his brother.

When he went to bed that night, he breathed a sigh of relief. To know that he was all right and right down the stairs if he needed anything made him happy with the bigger house and the furniture that was in it.

Waking up the next morning, the first thing he did was check on his brother. Since he was still sleeping, he let him go and went to the kitchen to find out what was around to eat. Having a cook was nice in that he didn't have to worry over meals or clean up afterwards. Just as he was finishing his second plate of pancakes, not only did Emma join him, but so did Kayce. It was a perfect way to start out the day with family.

Colby didn't have to go out today as it was his day off. Having Douglas around certainly made his life a great deal better. He could actually take a day off now and again and not have to worry so much about the trips. Today was the day he was to spend the day going over payroll and books while Emma was out on a short run. Having Kayce all to himself made him feel like he had the best of both worlds. Working and having family around when you wanted to hang out with them.

Having Kayce around made it harder for him to concentrate, but he finally got through everything that he needed to. By noon, not only had he gotten all the bills paid, but he had been able to look over two boats that he was considering purchasing one of. Also, he got the payroll sent into the company that fixed his check for him—they made sure that the deductions were taken out and the checks were written for his few employees.

The only other thing that he had to do was to go over to see Charlotte, Emma's mom, and help her with her new garden. She needed it tilled up so that she could have things planted. He'd learned how to use a tiller, like all his family knew how to do when he'd been living with his family before coming out here. Glad to do it for her, Kayce stayed at home to rest up while he went and did this for his mother-in-law.

Colby was nearly done with the big garden when Emma reached out to him. She said she'd be home around four and asked him if he wanted to have dinner in. Since he was in the mood for some comfort food, he asked if she wanted to go to Jack's with her mom and Kayce. She was all for the idea as she had been wanting comfort too. He thought it was great how their minds worked all the time. Whistling as he finished up the garden, he asked Charlotte if she wanted to go with them.

"I've been thinking about that all day, how much fun we had the last time we were there. Ask him first, though. I don't want to get my hopes up if he's already promised the table to one of the other family members. He might not have room for us." He did that right then and asked his brother if there was room for the four of them for dinner tonight. Jack said that he always held a table for one of them coming in, and he couldn't remember if anyone else had said they were going or not.

"No, no one has said anything to me. If you want the table, it's yours. Just try to come in early so that if you stay late, the kids are out of here sooner. They've been loving all this business that we've been generating. The tips are really good too." They both laughed, and Colby thanked him. "It's perfectly fine. Come in about five-thirty, and things will work out great. You know, even if there wasn't enough room tonight for you, I'd just slap another table onto it and you'd be eating with family. That would have been all right, too, right?"

"Perfectly fine with us." He reached out to Emma to let her know and then asked Kayce. He was excited to be eating there as well since he'd not been there since the first night, before he'd opened. *"Great. We'll leave around five-fifteen and have plenty of time to have dinner. This way, if he needs to, he can turn the table again after we leave. I'm hungry for some fried chicken and mashed potatoes now."*

"That sounds terrific. I loved the chicken. However, my favorite of all he does is the sliced fried cornbread. That's perfect with a few pieces of fried chicken." They both agreed they'd be getting that, and he let Emma and Charlotte know they were in. *"Since you wouldn't allow me to pay for dinner last night, I will tonight. It's the least I can do after you've been putting up with me all week so far."*

"Deal. I'll leave the tip." The two of them spoke off and on while he put in rows for Charlotte's garden. She was already putting in peas and carrots when he was cleaning up the tiller for when she needed it the next time. He was going to have to borrow hers when he put in his own garden. Colby couldn't wait until that happened.

The rest of the afternoon, he helped Charlotte put in her garden. He thought that she might well have been overdoing it, but he didn't say anything. It was just her living in the house, and the amount of carrots she was putting in the ground was enough to feed a small army. But she was having fun, and he couldn't have faulted her with that.

When Emma came over to her mom's house, she did have a little to say about how big the garden had turned out to be. But like him, she didn't say too much because her mom really was having some fun with it, and she was out in the sunshine too. He loved the outdoors too and was sure that's why the job that he had was so suited to him. He could be outside and on the ocean at the same time.

Tomorrow he was going to go out again, this time with his new crew. He'd hired nine people and was going to keep them on the payroll so that he could have them ready and trained when the time was right for him to buy the next boat. He was contemplating getting it in the next two weeks, which was about three months ahead of the schedule that he had for himself. Excitement tingled over his body when he thought of how well he was doing with nothing more than a boat and a crew.

He had noticed that the people he took out seemed to enjoy themselves even if they didn't catch anything but some smaller fish. It was when one of them caught something big — like the swordfish that had been caught two weeks ago — that the excitement would get going. They just seemed to have fun at what they were doing, and he was glad for that. So far, he'd not had any trouble with the fishing trips, and he was sure that a lot of that had to do with Parker putting something around him to keep himself and his crew safe. He'd certainly not had any calls like he did the one time.

They decided to dress up to go out to eat. Dressing up for him only meant that he wore a suit coat and tie. His jeans were brand-new, so he didn't have to wear dress pants. Mostly, all he ever wore was shorts and a company logo shirt with some sturdy tennis shoes. So it was nice to have to put on a tie and jacket for a change. Besides, he thought that Emma looked fantastic in her dress and heels. She certainly didn't look like the truck driver that she was.

Dinner was great, as usual. There was plenty enough to go around, and when the bill came, not nearly as much as it should have been, he left a generous tip for the girl who waited on them just as Jack told them to do. When they fed the family, they usually made enough on their tips to have a fantastic night. He supposed that's why they never got the same staff twice; Jack was spreading around the money like a good boss did.

~*~

Emma was glad to be home for the next three days. Her schedule was working out better than she could have wanted, and when she'd talked to Taylor about cutting back on her hours, she couldn't have been nicer. In fact, she told her that she'd gone down to two days a week, too, so that she could spend more time with Jack and her grannie.

"I've been thinking about going down to not coming in at all when the babies come. I want a lot of children. Mostly because I can afford them, and again, I want to be heavy with Jack's child. I think I might enjoy being a mom." She didn't say it, but she was betting that she was thinking of her own mom and how she'd treated her. "Did I tell you that they're changing prisons for my mom? She'll be in one that can be more helpful to her needs. She'll not be getting to be the center of attention, but she will be able to see a doctor who can get her out of the habit of thinking that she is. I doubt that it'll work, but then I don't really care so long as they don't let her out."

"They can't, can they? I mean, someone somewhere will have something to say about that, wouldn't they?" Taylor said that she didn't have a chance for parole, so that would help her stay inside. But the rest she'd not gotten involved in and wouldn't unless it was necessary. "Colby was telling me of some of the things that she did to you and Jack. I'm so sorry for that. It must have been difficult to be around her all the time. I don't know that I could have done it."

"It was all that I knew about her. She'd been that way my entire life. I think that's why I want to have children so badly, so I can love them like I was never loved." She said she could see that. "I knew that you would. You're a good friend, Emma. I'm so happy that we got to meet one another and become family. I wished for that when I met you. That you'd be one of the others' mates so that we could hang out with the other three."

"I'm so glad that I was Colby's mate, too. I didn't want him to be anywhere near me at first, but I find that I can't get enough of him when he's not around. I love him so much." She felt her face heat up a little for being so much in love with one person. "He rocks my world. I know that's an old saying, but it's just how he makes me feel when I'm around him."

The two of them talked about business and what they'd been doing around their new homes. She'd been having so much fun filling out their home that she couldn't wait for the last bit of furniture to arrive. Taylor said that she and Jack have been going to tag sales to find things to fill out the little places in their home. Then she told her about the teapot that she'd picked up recently.

"It's blue and green, but to say it like that sounds so boring. It's beautifully made, and the little teacups that go with it are so delicate and fragile-looking. There are cream and sugar containers that go with it, too. I guess I should be calling it a tea set, not just a teapot. I love using it when it's just me, and when my grannie gets back the day after tomorrow, I'm going to have a nice cup of tea with her too." She asked how her grannie was enjoying the cruise. "I don't believe she is. Not toward the end of it anyway. I think she misses everyone here. That's what she mostly talks about when we chat."

"She's been gone a month, right?" Taylor said she'd been gone just a little over that in that it would be thirty-eight days when she finally returned home. "I know that I couldn't do a cruise for that long. I'd be missing everyone, too. It would be like I've lost my family for too long or something like that."

"I know I could do it if it were just myself and Jack." Emma said that would be different if it were just her and Colby. "Yes, I know it would be. For all we'd be hanging out with the other people on the cruise, we might as well be all alone on the big thing."

"It would be so romantic to just be the two of us. I think I'd love that. No phone calls or business. No long hours in a truck. Yes, I could do that easily. Just the two of us on the ocean would be fantastic. So long as I don't get seasick. That would really suck." The two of them laughed, saying that it would be just like them to be the only people to get sick on an ocean liner while on a romantic trip with their husbands. "We should do that. All of us go on a trip like that. Before the babies come. I know that Ivy is already having a baby, but we could go on this trip one time before we don't have time because of the children."

"I think that's a wonderful idea. Not for a month, though. Too much is going on for us to be gone that long. But at least a week would be great." They started planning it right then. It would be expensive, but so worth it. They were looking up prices and times they could go before the meeting for her next client came in. Emma went home that night with a list of things she was supposed to pick up. They were even going to try to convince their grandparents to go with them. It would be so much fun.

She'd spoken to Colby and Kayce about it last night, and they were both for it. Kayce was a little worried about his business and taking another week off, but he said he didn't care; the other partners took time off all the time to go on trips with their families.

Emma had thought that Colby wouldn't want to take a cruise, as he was on the ocean almost every day. But he told her that he was usually working when he was out, and to be on a cruise wouldn't be nearly the same. He'd have fun being out on the water where someone else was in charge.

Since everyone agreed it would be a blast, all they needed to do was pick a date to leave and return. They were pushing for two weeks, not because they thought that it would be less than a month, but because they deserved it. And she thought that if anyone did, it would be this family. They'd given up so much just to be here in another state, but they had also worked so hard to be what they had become, too.

"Are you ready for bed?" She'd forgotten for a second where she was and smiled at Colby. "You looked lost there for a moment. Is everything all right? You don't need me to slay any dragons for you, do you?"

"No, not tonight." She wrapped her arms around his shoulders and looked up at him. He was such a handsome man that she would often wonder how she'd ended up with him. "I would like for you to make love to me tonight. I know that your brother has gone back to his place now, and we'll have the entire house to ourselves."

"I'd very much love to make love to you. Anytime or anyplace." He kissed her then, taking her breath away with how thorough it was. "How about if I lock up and you go upstairs and get into bed. I'll be up in a few minutes."

Excitement rolled over her. As soon as she was in the bedroom, she had to decide what to wear and decided that nothing would be just fine for what she had in mind. She wanted to suck on his cock and have him come all over her.

When he came into the room, she was standing in the middle of the room with nothing on but some perfume that she had put behind her knees. She thought that he was disappointed because he stood so long at the door that she thought he was going to go out again. When she moved toward him, he told her to stop.

"I want to have a look at the wonderment that is you. I love you, Emma Tucker, so very much." She said that she loved him as well and turned around when he asked her to. "Christ, how did I get so lucky as to have someone like you in my life as my wife and partner for all time? I can't believe my luck. I consider myself to be the luckiest man in the world to have you."

"Come to bed with me." He nodded and closed the door. The turning of the lock startled her, then made her wet when she thought about what that meant. He didn't want anyone to bother them, and she was all right with that. "Sit here on the edge. I've been thinking about you all day and having your cock in my mouth." His hissed breath made her smile.

Stripping him down to his briefs had her mouth watering. When his cock was peeking over the top of them, she licked the tiny hole that was there and sighed heavily. This was exactly what she wanted from him.

Pulling his pants down to his ankles, then off, she was surprised at how hard he was. Taking his cock into her hands, she massaged him as she worked her mouth around his crown. He was so thick that she wondered if she could take him, but decided that she would even if it was painful. Colby was hers, and she was going to make sure that he knew it.

Bobbing her head over him, she could taste his cum as it leaked from the tip. Following the thick vein from tip to root, she was rewarded by his cock brushing against her throat. Taking him into her mouth, she had to relax her jaw bones so that he could slip into the back of her throat and beyond. Gagging just for a moment, Emma swallowed around him and heard his quick intake of breath when she did that to him.

Letting him fuck her mouth, she played with his balls. They were hot and heavy, and she loved the way that they felt when she rolled them around in her hands. When he put his hand on her head, moving her hair out of the way so that she could see him, Emma loved to watch him throw back his head and close his eyes. It was as if it was all too much for him, and he just didn't know how to control himself. She didn't want control; she wanted him to come with her. But he had other things in mind.

Sliding her hand down her breast to her pussy, she could feel the wetness of it as she touched her clit. Nearly coming, she moaned long and hard and felt the way he loved it. Pulling her up and off his cock, he fisted himself and came. Hitting her lips and face with his cum she touched her clit again and came screaming his name as he covered her with himself.

"I can't move." She giggled a little, her heart beating hard enough that she was sure that he could hear it. "Baby, I want to take you, but I'm afraid that if I move, I'm going to fall on my face. I'm spent."

"I enjoyed that as well." He did move then and moaned loudly. When he fell back on the bed, his body about as limp as she'd ever seen him, she got up off the floor and went to the bathroom. Cleaning herself up, she nearly came again when she saw how she looked in the bathroom mirror. When she came back to the bedroom, Colby was lying in the middle of the bed with the sheets pulled up to his chest. He asked her how she was doing.

"Fantastic. Great. Amazing." He laughed with her and asked her to come to bed. "I will. I want to be held by you for the rest of the night."

"I can do that." Once she was in bed, he pulled her beneath him. When his cock was at her entrance, she nearly begged him to take her, and he did. With his cock deep inside of her, his mouth on her breasts, she held onto him like the lifeline that he was. He was her everything.

He made love to her slowly. Her releases, several of them, were mind-blowing and gentle at the same time. She came so many times that she was sure that she was going to be sore again in the morning. If nothing else, she knew that she was loved by Colby and loved that no matter what, he was there for her.

When he came with her, she held onto him tightly. Even as she started to black out from exhaustion, she told him that she loved him. Tomorrow would be a wonderful day simply because he was with her and they loved one another. Emma thought that she could spend the rest of her life in bed with him and never have a single regret.

Chapter 10

Molly looked up when the nurse came into the room. They'd not seen the doctor in a couple of days, but she wasn't worried. They'd been told that he had to take a few days off from being hurt, and she knew firsthand that he'd been popped in the nose. She felt sort of bad about how she'd treated him when he'd been in to see her Pop-Pop.

"You thinking on that doctor again? I told you that he's the best there is and he ain't gonna hold it against you for being upset with him." She said she'd been rude to him. "He won't see it that way. He'll just say you'd been worried, and he didn't help matters any by being hurt like he was. You just stop that thinking like you are before you're in the bed next to me. Not that I'd mind all that much, but I'd have you right there with me."

She patted him on the hand like she did when he was right. Which, to her way of thinking, he usually was. Just as she was going to tell him that she was going to tell the man she was sorry for being such a bitch, her father walked in and slapped her off the chair.

"Why would you go and do that for? She's done nothing wrong, William Toby. You help her up." He said he wasn't going to do no such thing and was pissed off at her. "Whatever for? She's been sitting right here by my side since I took that tumble five days ago. I'm going home today, and she's already made arrangements for me to get there."

Molly got herself up off the floor with enough distance between her and her father so he'd not be able to hit her again. As it was now, she had a bloody mouth, and there was blood coming from her nose. It would be just like her father to have no reason at all for knocking her around. He just liked to show people that he was the one in charge. Even if he wasn't.

"She didn't tell me where you were. I should have been the first person she called before the police, even." Pop-Pop said that she'd called him an ambulance just like she should have done. "No, you're my father, and I should have been in on the decision whether or not you went to the hospital. That's the way it should have been."

"You fool, and what kind of words of wisdom would you have had with me banged up the way I was? And I told her to call the ambulance on account of me hurting like I'd broken my leg or something. Not to mention hitting my head on that rail that I asked you to fix for me several times." Dad said he'd been busy. "Too busy to help out your old man. Did you ever think that I might not have wanted you around me when I was in so much pain? You never see the whole picture when it's right there in your face, do you, son? Where are those boys of yours? They in jail again?"

"One of them is." Dad eyed her. "You got blood on your face. You should clean it up." She was afraid to turn her back on him for fear of what he'd do to her when she did. She knew better than to show him her back so that he could stick a knife in it sometimes. "Wash your face, damn it, before I give you something else to wash off."

That was another thing about her dad. He wasn't the least bit smart. Not clever, nor was he very kind. She doubted every time she saw him that he'd be alive the next day. He didn't suffer fools well, and he was the biggest one that she knew. And for the most part, she hated him with every fiber of her being.

He'd never been there for her. When she'd been living at home with him and her brothers, she was the cook, cleaning lady, and laundry person. Also, she was a slave to whatever kind of shit they got themselves into. So when she turned eighteen, with the advice of her grandfather, she joined the service and never came home when they would know about it. All her time was spent with her Pop-Pop and no one else.

"You got any money on you?" She told him that all she had was a few bucks to get herself something to eat later. "Well, hand it over. I've not had anything to eat today worth shit, and you'll just have to do for yourself."

"No." She'd been getting really good at telling him no, too. Since the last time she'd seen him, he'd been taking her money, and she wasn't going to have it. "I said that it's for me. You have a job, don't you? Or have you pissed that one away, too?"

He lunged at her, and she didn't move. If he could have heard her heart beating, he would have known that she was terrified out of her skin, but so far all he'd done was to make a fool of himself in front of his father. Pop-Pop wouldn't allow him to hit her the second time without him hurting her dad.

Slipping into the bathroom that held her purse, she took out all the cash she had on her, about one hundred and seventy dollars, and put it in one of the rolls of toilet tissue. She kept the two ones she had on herself. It wouldn't do for him to catch her lying to him, but if she had money on her, he'd take every penny of it and knock her around because it wasn't more.

Coming out of the bathroom, she heard Pop-Pop yelling at her dad. She knew that her dad had asked him for money by the way the conversation was going. He'd asked his son if he thought that he had money in his underwear, as that was all that he had on besides the hospital gown. She might well have laughed if she weren't afraid of drawing attention to herself. It was then that the doctor from the other day came into the room.

"What the ever-loving hell is going on in here? I can hear you arguing all the way down to the nurses' station. You there, who are you?" Dad told Doctor Tucker he was William Toby, son of the man in the bed. "I'll not have you upsetting my patient, so you either keep it down or I'll have you escorted out of here."

"You go ahead and try that fancy boy, and I'll knock you on your ass." Dad was yelling again, so Doc just punched him in the face, knocking him to the floor. "You can't hit me. It's against the Geneva Convention for you to do something like that."

"The what?" Dad tried to explain that he'd taken an oath about not hurting anyone else while he was a doctor. "I see. It's called the Hippocratic Oath, nothing to do with

Geneva or any conventions. You don't read much, do you?"

"I read the sports page in the paper, and it's served me well." Doc just ignored him in favor of Pop-Pop. "What's wrong with him? And if there are any decisions to be made about him going to a nursing home, I'm going to be the one to sign him in. He should have died off a long time ago."

Again, he was ignored, and Molly thought it was just what he deserved. As Doc was asking her grandfather how he was doing, she noticed her dad was looking for something. More than likely, her purse but it was still in the bathroom. Not that he would go in there, something else about her father is that he was a germophobic when it came to bathrooms and the germs that might be in them, especially in a hospital setting.

"He ain't going home today. I got plans for his house now that I know he ain't there." The doc said he'd be the one making that decision, and he was going home today. "Well, it'll have to be tonight. I have me some searching to do, and it's better when he ain't there distracting me all the time."

"If you're looking for money, I've done cashed my check and paid my bills with it. You want something more than money, I ain't got that either. You just keep your hands off my stuff, you idiot, or I'll make what the doc here did to you look like a swat with a fly swatter." Dad said he couldn't talk to him like that. "Yet here I am talking to you like that. You're a fool. Besides, don't think I didn't notice that you didn't say anything about your job. You lost another one, didn't you?"

"They didn't care for me sleeping on the job. Idiots should know that when a man works the night shift, he's going to have to take a nap now and again. They didn't pay me enough to do that job anyway. Who needs to have security when it's just dog food I'm protecting?" Pop-Pop said it might have been for the people working there. "Nah, they're not smart enough to have nobody chasing after them for the little bit they paid me."

"You never did make any sense when you were talking out the side of your mouth, did you, son? I swear to Christ, your momma must have had her babies switched out when you were born. There is no way that you are a part of us." Dad said he wasn't no baby no more. "See? That's just what I'm talking about. Dumber than a sack of rocks you are. Go on home and leave me to my stay here. I got better things to do than to listen to you spout off about how you ain't supposed to nap on a job. Nobody naps on the job, you old fool. It's not what they're paying you for."

"Whatever, Dad. You just go on thinking what you want. I know better." Dad looked at her. "Where is that couple of bucks you're going to give over to me?"

"I told you no. I'm keeping it to myself." He said for her to show him, and she knew that trick from him. He'd just take it. "I don't need to show you what I have or don't have. I have a couple of bucks for my dinner, and that's all you're going to have to know. And you ever hit me again, and I'll be all over your ass. I'm not a kid anymore. I've been trained on how to protect myself."

"Says she who had a bloody mouth." Dad laughed

like he'd just thought up the funniest joke. "We'll see about that money you got. You have to leave this room at some point, and I'm going to be right there waiting on your ass. See that I don't."

"I don't." Dad looked confused, and she didn't explain to him what she'd meant. Sometimes she would mess with him about stuff like that just to see him looking in his usual state of confusion. Doc asked to see her mouth. "It's fine. I've had worse. Just see to my Pop-Pop so he can get out of here."

After a few seconds of him just staring at her, she turned away from him. There was something very tense about the way he was looking at her, and she didn't like it. She didn't like him either. Not that he was like her father, no, he'd never hit first without a reason, but he was intense. Like something was going on that he wasn't all that thrilled about. Sitting in the chair when he turned his back to her, she felt like her knees just gave out. Like his staring at her was some sort of battle, and she'd not come out on top.

"I'm sorry that you had to stay those extra two days, Mr. Toby. But the men watching over you while I was out for those few days didn't know what I had planned and ordered you to stay." Her grandfather had said it was all right that he'd been able to visit with his favorite granddaughter. She pointed out that she was his only granddaughter, and like the old joke went, he laughed. "Well, I'll get you out of here today. Do you have a ride?"

"I rented a car so that I could get back and forth from here." She told him it was no problem as she'd been going to rent one anyway to get around when she came to visit him. "I needed one anyway."

After he was discharged, her father finally got it through his head that he wasn't in charge at the hospital, and leaving, she loaded her grandfather up in her rental and took him home. On the way, they stopped for his prescriptions and something they could eat when they got there. Dad wouldn't come over with his dad at home; he knew better. Pop-Pop would knock the shit out of him even if he was banged up.

She'd picked up one of the rotisserie chickens at the store, and that's what the two of them had with a bag of some sweet rolls. It was filling, delicious, and easy to eat. That's what they wanted, too. No mess, no fuss.

Pop-Pop was getting around better than he'd been when he'd first gotten to the hospital, so that was good. Getting him in his chair was easy as he walked to it and sat himself down. All she needed to do was give him the remote so that they could watch Jeopardy together and enjoy being at home. She left to go back in two days, and neither of them talked about it.

After another game show, he was dozing, so she helped him get his jammies on and get his teeth brushed. He was tired after the ride home and getting around, so she didn't fuss at him too much. Once he was in bed, she went to the living room again and watched a little television while he snored in the other room. She loved not just her grandfather, but she also loved this old house.

Her grandparents had lived here all her life. When her grannie had been alive, it seemed to be brighter and more friendly. She knew that Grannie was the reason that they even had this old house; Grannie had been the one to pay the bills when it came time, and she kept the lights on and the furnace running, too. After she died, she'd had to train her grandfather how to pay his bills online and to get them set up so he was forever with money. She kept an eye on his funds, too, so that whenever he would be short for whatever reason, she'd put money in his account because she knew that he'd do the same for her.

They were a pair, the two of them, and she'd walk to the ends of the earth for him. He'd do the same for her, too. However, it was her father that she had to watch out for. He was stupid sure, but he was also as mean as a feral cat that hadn't eaten in a couple of days. And just like that cat, she knew to avoid him as much as possible.

~*~

It came as no surprise to Colby that the bank approved him for the boat loan. They knew how much money was being put into his account weekly and what the money was from. All he needed to do was to find the second boat that he wanted, have it rigged out, and put it on the water. That was the fun part, having the boat rigged up to what he wanted it to look like. He'd been doing this long enough that he knew just what was needed and not needed in the way of fishing boats.

He'd worked for years for another fishing company while they lived at home. He would usually be the one who took the boats out on the water and stayed with the people who were fishing. They didn't have nearly all the amenities that he had because he paid attention to what was being said and done on the boats.

For instance, they had to bring their own food on their trips. There were no sandwiches given to the fishermen, nor was there the opportunity to have a place to dine should they want it. While the dining part had never come to fruition, it had been an option for them if they wanted it.

There was no liquor on his boats unless they brought it on themselves and signed a waiver saying that they'd pay for any damages made to the boat and crew. That usually deterred them from bringing aboard anything other than a few beers. He'd seen firsthand what that sort of drinking could do while in the middle of the ocean.

Colby decided he was going to take his time with this one. Get it the way that he wanted it and take it out on a maiden voyage before using it for fishing. He'd made that mistake, though a small one, when he'd purchased the boat that he had now. It had been minor but no less annoying when the first boat had no mattresses for its beds when they went out. Lucky for the crew, it had only been a single night's stay out, or it might have been worse.

Getting in his car, he was headed to the marina when he heard from his brother-in-law, David Manchester, married to his sister, Dakota. Not hearing all that often from David, they talked about things before he got down to business.

"I wanted to borrow your brother's restaurant for a day, and he said that I needed to clear it with you first. Something about making sandwiches for your trip. I can do that for you."

He said that he didn't have a trip out for the next two days, but Jack usually supplied him with sandwiches. *"That would be easy, as that's what I'm doing. We've been asked to cater a meal for one hundred and fifty people. Just sandwiches, and we'd have more room at the restaurant. It's on a Monday and I know that he's not open on those days."*

"Go ahead and use it if he's all right with you doing so. As I said, I don't have anything going out on Monday that would require any sandwiches. It's only a few hours out and back. It was something that I picked up for Donald so that he could get used to those kinds of trips." David asked him how well things were going. *"I'm headed to the harbor to pick out another boat for the business. That's how wonderful it's going."*

"Congratulations. That's wonderful news. Kota and I have been so busy that we've not had much contact with the family lately. We're going to have to get out more. But our business is really picking up, too. I can't believe how well we're doing." Colby told him that he was proud of him and glad things were taking off so well. *"Yeah, I can't believe it. It was the hand up that we got from the foundation, or we'd still be working a nine-to-five job without any chance of branching out into our own business. Kota and I are talking about having children again."*

"Grandda and grannie will be thrilled to know that part." He could tell that David was laughing and knew how he felt about being so happy that the foundation had helped them out. *"I'm in awe that things are finally working out for us all. And only because of Denver taking a chance by getting in contact with Ronin. I'll be singing his praises for the rest of my life."*

"*Me too.*" Laughing again, the two of them closed the connection, and Colby pulled into the first parking lot that he saw. Things were busy on the harbor, and he couldn't wait to be a part of the excitement that was there. People loved the docks, and so did he.

After talking to three dealerships, he made his way to someplace to eat. The harbor had all kinds of food, and he had his heart set on something with seafood. Of course he did, laughing to himself. Entering the first one he came to, he ordered their seafood special for the day and sat at one of the outside tables to enjoy it. While doing that, he looked over the paperwork he'd collected and the brochures he'd picked up, too. An hour later, he was back to visiting the stores that he'd visited over the last few weeks.

"*How much longer do you think you're going to be?*" He grinned when he heard from Emma; she sounded so stressed out. "*I have a flat, and while I'm not asking you to fix it for me, I have a crew on their way to do that, I'm bored out of my mind, and going to be two hours before they get here and another hour or so before they get me back on the road.*"

"*I'm sorry.*" He sat down on one of the many benches that were along the seafront. Watching the water coming in and out, he told Emma what he was doing. "*It's got to be better than what you're seeing. Where are you anyway?*"

She told him. "*So as you might well know, I'm looking at a highway that goes to my next store, and I'm sitting in my truck. At least it has air conditioning. It's supposed to be really warm today.*" He told her that he was sorry again. "*I want to have dinner tonight at home. I want something to grill out.*"

I should have said something to Parker about grilling out. She might have put me in an entire picnic area in my rig so that I could enjoy it."

"*That sounds like something she'd do.*" They talked about Parker and her incredible magic. "*I know that she fixed our houses so that no one can enter with having ill will in their heart. I had to ask someone what that meant, and I love that she did that.*"

Colby sat on the bench for the next two and a half hours talking to Emma. They laughed and talked about the house. Then she told him about her own mom. She'd died of cancer when she'd only been twenty-eight, and Emma was only two and had been left to be raised by her dad. Then he'd died after meeting Charlotte.

He'd forgotten that Charlotte wasn't her real mother but the daughter of her father. The two of them were closer than mother and daughter, and he loved them both. Grief could bring even the worst people together, and he was glad that they'd found one another to hold onto in their moments of need.

"*Well, they're here now and not soon enough for me. I thought that I'd just bother you a bit, and we've been talking the entire time. I'm sorry.*" He told her that he was glad that he could help her. "*But you didn't get to get your boat today. I know you were looking forward to that.*"

"*What? Are you kidding? Getting to talk to you all afternoon could have been my entire day and not just a couple of hours. I love talking to you. Sometimes I miss you so much that this really helps when I'm down and out.*" She asked him if he got that way often. "*Not too often. Especially now that you're a part of my life. You make me happy, and all I need to do is think about you, and I get in a better mood than I was before. I love you so very much."*

"*And I love you so much, too.*" She said that she needed to make sure these guys got her fixed up well, and she needed to get going after that. *"I love talking to you, but I can't do it when I'm driving. It's too much of a distraction.*

"*It is for me too when I'm on the boat.*" They talked a bit more, then he got up and started for the docks again. He wanted to get the boat today to have it started on to be upgraded, but now he was distracted. All he wanted to do was go home and wait for Emma to come back. She said she'd be late coming home, and he knew that he'd wait up for her.

Not that his trip to buy a boat was ruined, far from it. He'd got to spend some time with the love of his life while she was stranded. And it had been fun too for him. Talking about anything and everything under the sun together. He thought that they could do that more often, but only when they weren't doing their jobs. It could be dangerous for both of them. She could have an accident, and he could fall off the boat or cause harm to one of his crew members or the clients.

Going back to the place that he purchased the first one from, Colby ordered his boat and then talked about the upgrades. All he really needed done was the crew sleeping area to have bunk beds put in on either side of the walls and extra seating around the fishing dock.

Colby arrived home about an hour later than he had expected to. Dinner was going to be late again but he didn't mind. The two of them had been eating around eight o'clock for the past couple of weeks. Then they'd head up to bed around midnight. It was late getting to bed for the two of them, but they didn't care. His grandda had told him that he was young yet and could afford to not sleep a full night. But he also cautioned not to do it too often, as it would make them very ill. What he actually said was that it would make them old before their time.

Getting the grill ready for dinner, when Emma told him that she was in town, the two of them met out on the deck to have dinner out there. Along with the steaks, they were having a green salad and a baked potato. The warm bread was from Jack's place that he had left over, and they were going to make good use of it, sopping up the juices from the steaks.

"When are you going to your grandparents again? If it's on my days off, I'd love to go with you." He said that he was supposed to go tomorrow so that he could take his grandda to the dentist. "Well, that would be all right if I miss that. But the next time you go over to work, I want to go too. It'll be nice to see them again."

"It's my turn to mow the lawn. He had a service do it, but that boy went off to college. I think he's avoiding grandda. He had to get a little shitty with him about being paid while not working." That was a funny story, and he told her about it just like his grandda did to him. "Neither the boy nor his dad ever said a word to him again. I thought that I'd laugh my butt off."

"He is a good man, your grandda. And I love your grannie. She's funny in a slick sort of way. Like, there are times when I don't know if she's insulting someone or giving them a compliment. I don't know that the person she's talking to knows either." He said that Grannie could and would peel the skin right off your hide if she thought that you needed it. "I know. I heard her fussing with Denver the other day. She never raised her voice, nor did she curse once, but I thought that he was going to cry; he was so upset. I feel like that sometimes when I disappoint my grannie. She never says much, but I know that I have, and it hurts me to my heart. I hate that feeling."

"Once when I was little, Grannie caught me in a lie. I don't remember what it was about, I just remember that I had lied to her about something, and she knew it. When confronted with the evidence that I was lying, I stood there with my chin held high and waited for her to spank me. She would do that, too, spank us when we needed it. Anyway, she told me that she was disappointed in me for lying and that I shouldn't do that again because it hurt her heart. I cried for a solid three days over that. She was disappointed in me first of all, but because it had been her that I'd lied to her, that hurt too. I remember what it was now. I'd taken cookies from the countertop where she'd been cooling them. They were going to be Christmas gifts for some of the neighborhood families, and I'd messed up her counting. I never take anything from their home unless I ask from then on. And especially not any cookies anymore."

"I want to spank our children when they need it. I've seen too many kids who need their asses whipped when they talk back to their parents, and I don't think it's something like abuse. It's abuse to me if you don't make sure your kids know right from wrong." He agreed with her. "All right. When can we have these kids? I want to be having your baby soon."

"How about tonight we create one?" She raced him to the bedroom, nearly falling down the first stairs that she went up. Colby was laughing so hard that he nearly fell himself. "Be careful, love. You don't want to break anything tonight."

Before You Go...

HELP AN AUTHOR

write a review

THANK YOU!

Share your voice and help guide other readers to these wonderful books. Even if it's only a line or two your reviews help readers discover the author's books so they can continue creating stories that you'll love. Login to your favorite retailer and leave a review. Thank you.

AWARD WINNING, BESTSELLING AUTHOR

Kathi S. Barton is an award-winning and bestselling author known for her steamy paranormal romances and unforgettable characters. A recipient of the prestigious Pinnacle Book Achievement Award, her books have topped the charts on Amazon and All Romance eBooks, earning her a loyal global readership.

Kathi lives in Nashport, Ohio, with her husband, Paul. When she's not crafting passionate love stories set in magical worlds, she enjoys camping, exploring local auctions, and attending county fairs, where Paul showcases his artwork and pottery. Her creative spark—fueled by a muse she describes as a cross between Jimmy Stewart and Hugh Jackman—brings her stories to vivid, heartfelt life.

Paranormal romance with plenty of heat is her favorite genre, and she loves connecting with her readers. Feel free to reach out—Kathi would love to hear from you.

Email: aaronskiss@gmail.com
Blog: kathisbartonauthor.blogspot.com